"Still a ne[...]

The handsome baby-sitter grinned when Maddie handed the crying baby back to him.

"I'm not a mom. Timmy's on loan, and he scares me. I'm glad I could get a sitter on such short notice."

"Oh, come on. Hold him." At his urging she did. "Relax, though. Babies can pick up all sorts of vibes." He rested his hand on her shoulder. "Just like adults can."

A tiny shiver went through Maddie at his touch. He was *so* gorgeous!

"See. You're tense." He gently massaged her shoulder, but that only made her more tense. "Maybe we ought to take care of you first." He placed Timmy in bed. "After all, you had a rough time getting home in that snowstorm."

"Please don't come on to me." Maddie couldn't get her voice much above a whisper. "I've had a lousy night. And somewhere in this city there's a man called **Michael Harrington** who is, no doubt, having a lousy night, too. Chances are he's holding me responsible."

"No, he's not, Maddie," he insisted, his lips close to hers. "Allow me to introduce myself."

Like many authors, **Elise Title** thinks writing a book is akin to going through labor. And she knows what she's talking about because she and her husband have two children. Elise was certainly happy to "deliver" *Baby, It's You!*, her second Temptation, and a tender, warmhearted fantasy. "Many of the heroine's experiences with 'her first baby' are similar to my own," she says, "and it was fun to relive the wonder of it."

Elise has thirty novels to her credit under the name Alison Tyler. The Title family lives in Hanover, New Hampshire.

Books by Elise Title

HARLEQUIN TEMPTATION
203–LOVE LETTERS

HARLEQUIN INTRIGUE
97–CIRCLE OF DECEPTION

Baby, It's You!

ELISE TITLE

Harlequin Books

TORONTO • NEW YORK • LONDON
AMSTERDAM • PARIS • SYDNEY • HAMBURG
STOCKHOLM • ATHENS • TOKYO • MILAN

Published October 1988

ISBN 0-373-25323-0

1

MADDIE SARGENT GRIPPED the phone, quivering in rage, her knuckles white.

"Yes," she said tightly. "That's exactly what I said. It shrank."

She listened to the clerk at the other end of the line for only a moment before her rage heightened. "I could have swallowed a horse for lunch and the dress wouldn't be this tight. And more to the point, I did not ask to have the dress dry-cleaned. I said pressed. Pressed. It's brand-new. I've never even worn it. It was just a bit creased, that's all. I bought this dress expressly for a very important dinner meeting tonight. The last thing I need at this moment is this kind of aggravation."

In the midst of her tirade the doorbell rang. She dragged the phone across the living room and went to see who was there. "Oh, what's the use," she muttered into the receiver. "I don't have time to argue about it now."

At the door she took a quick look through the peephole and then opened it with her free hand. A plump young woman entered, giving Maddie a wry smile as she scanned her outfit. Maddie raised her hazel eyes toward the ceiling and strode back to the telephone table, talking all the way. "I'll be down to see the manager of your dry-cleaning establishment first thing Monday morning. And you might inform him that this dress cost me two hundred and thirty-four dollars, and I intend to get full reparation."

Maddie hung up the phone, her outraged expression turning to despair as she stared down at her dress and then across to her friend and administrative assistant, Liz Cooper.

"It shrank," Liz said with a humorous grimace.

"I know I'm foolishly superstitious—" Maddie sighed "—but something tells me the Fates are trying to warn me of bad tidings."

Liz grinned. "Buck up. I've actually managed to get a bit of helpful information for you on our Mr. Harrington."

Maddie returned a halfhearted smile. "Good. You can fill me in while I try to dig up something else to wear." She walked into her bedroom and wriggled out of the red jersey dress that had once fit her lithe, one hundred and fifteen pound, five-foot-five body to perfection. It would now look better on a scrawny ten-year-old.

Liz followed, watching Maddie pull dresses out of her closet, frown and then hang them up again.

"How about that little black number you wore to the Christmas party last month?" Liz suggested, slipping off her blue down parka.

"You mean the one that our eminent dermatologist, Kevin Gleason, spilled punch on?" Maddie slipped on a gray crepe de chine, took a quick look in the mirror and immediately proceeded to strip it off.

Liz smiled at her attractive, blond-haired boss. "Maddie, relax. I've never seen you so frazzled. You'll look terrific in whatever you wear. And you'll do great with Harrington."

"Need I remind you, Liz Cooper, how crucial this deal is? If we land this new line of skin-care products for a luxury chain like Barrett's, it's not only going to mean fabulous visibility for the whole Sargent line, but it will also put an end to all our cash-flow and reinvestment worries. This undercapitalized baby of mine that I've nursed through infancy and seven years of growing pains just might finally be able to start standing on its own two feet."

"Look, Maddie, no one knows better than me how hard you've worked to make Sargent one of the finest companies of its kind around. You're twenty-eight and look how far you've come in seven years. Okay, we're small, but we've got a fabulous product line and a dedicated staff. Harrington is going to be bowled over. Besides, Barrett's came to us with the idea for this exclusive, not the other way around. I'll bet anything Harrington's up here to talk turkey."

Maddie grinned. "You're right. I should be optimistic. I need to get a grip on myself. This is just so important." She held up a cognac-colored wool dress.

Liz nodded. "That's a good one."

"I'll need to press the skirt a bit," she said, examining it. "Okay, tell me about Harrington."

Liz pulled a small notepad out of her purse. "Let's see. Harrington, Michael. Thirty-four years old. Single. Worked his way up the ranks at Barrett's to VP in charge of Marketing and New Product Development. A real Horatio Alger, it seems. Rumor has it he started out as a stock boy at the Barrett's store here in Boston." She flicked a page in a businesslike fashion. "He grew up here in Beantown, by the way. South End. Large family. He's the oldest. There's a sister at Wellesley College and a brother at Tufts. Premed. Three sisters who are

married. Oh, and there's another sister who's getting
married over in Watertown next Sunday. Harrington
will be staying in town for the week to attend the nup-
tials."

"How did you manage to dig all that up on two days'
notice?"

"I have an old college buddy who works in person-
nel at the Barrett's store here."

Maddie smiled. "What would I do without you?"

"Go insane probably."

Maddie laughed. "You're right." She bent down and
started searching for her black pumps. "Where did
Harrington go to school?"

"He never went to college. I do believe he's the only
top exec at Barrett's who doesn't have a fancy business
degree from some prestigious university. He rose to VP
the blood, sweat and tears way."

Maddie tossed one black pump into the room but
continued searching for its mate.

"You'd better wear boots," Liz said. "It's starting to
snow."

"Oh, great."

"Actually—" Liz hesitated "—they're predicting a
possible blizzard by late tonight."

"Wonderful. Harrington would have to choose Simeoni's clear across town for dinner," Maddie said as
she slipped on her flannel robe.

"At least Simeoni's has valet parking."

"If I can get my car started. It doesn't like cold
weather any more than I do." She glanced at her watch.
"Damn, look at the time. I've got to step on it, or I'll be
late."

"I've got to dash off, too. I've got to go to that baby
shower for my sister-in-law tonight."

"What's this baby? Number three?"

Liz laughed. "Four."

Maddie shook her head. "And I think *I* have my hands full."

Liz grabbed her parka and headed for the door. "Well, I'm off. Good luck. I'll speak to you tomorrow."

"Thanks again, Liz." Maddie saw Liz out and then hurried to the kitchen with her dress to set up the ironing board and plug in the iron.

Leaving the iron to heat up, she ran into the bathroom to comb her hair and apply some of her favorite Sargent moisturizing lotion, a light Sargent foundation, a touch of green eye shadow and a peach-toned lipstick.

She was back in the kitchen a couple of minutes later, fretting because the iron was still cold, when the doorbell rang insistently.

"Okay, okay. Hold on a minute," she shouted, giving the iron one frustrated scowl before she set it down and rushed for the door.

A cacophony of knocks and muted sobs accompanied the shrill, persistent rings.

"What the . . . ?" Maddie peered quickly through the peephole and then hastily flung open the door. Her cousin Linda was standing there, her infant son, Timmy, bundled up in her arms. It was Timmy doing the crying at the moment, but tears were rolling down the young woman's wan face. Her reddened eyes indicated that she'd been crying for a while.

"Good heavens, Linda. What is it? What's happened?" Maddie tried to usher her cousin inside, but the distraught woman wouldn't budge.

"It's Donald. He's gone."

Maddie gasped. "Gone?"

"He's . . . left me, Maddie. He's left me and Timmy."
As soon as she got the words out, Linda began crying
in earnest along with her infant.

"Oh, Linda," Maddie said, feeling at a complete loss,
"that's awful."

"Don . . . went to Vale, Colorado . . . for an engineer-
ing conference. He . . . he was supposed to be back this
morning. Only...he called and said he wants a...trial
separation. It's Timmy... the pressures of being a father . . . it's all so different since the baby . . ."

Maddie missed half of what Linda was saying because of the infant's bellowing, but she got the gist of
it. "Look, come inside and sit down for a while. I'm
afraid I have to rush out for a meeting. I'm late already.
But you stay here, and . . . and we'll talk later . . . when
I get back."

Linda remained firmly planted in the hallway. "I must
go to him and try to save my marriage, Maddie."

Before Maddie could respond, Linda thrust the
wailing baby into her arms.

"You've got to look after Tim . . . just for a couple of
days. There's no one else I can turn to."

"But...but...I can't," Maddie stammered, her voice
drowned out by the baby's shrieks, heightened now
that he found himself being held awkwardly in strange
arms. She tried to give him back to his mother, but
Linda was reaching down for a small overnight bag and
a plaid canvas car bed.

"Here. Timmy's clothes, bottles, some diapers, and
he can sleep in this," she said rapidly between quick,
shallow breaths, dumping the tote and car bed at Maddie's feet. "Oh, God, Maddie, I can't tell you what a
lifesaver you are. What would I ever have done without you? I love him so, Maddie. And Timmy needs his

father. It's just...such an adjustment. For me, too." She clutched Maddie's shoulder. "I'll be back Monday morning. I'll repay you somehow. I have to hurry. I've got just enough time to catch my plane."

After a quick hug that encompassed both Timmy and Maddie, Linda was gone.

The door swung shut in Maddie's stunned face. A moment later Maddie jerked the door back open only to witness the elevator doors sliding closed. Maddie stared down the empty hall and then at the screeching baby in her arms.

Panic set in. It was bad enough that she didn't know the slightest thing about babies. But of all the times in the world, there couldn't be a worse one than this to have to start learning. "No, no, this can't be happening. I don't believe this."

Poor Timmy seemed none too happy with the situation, either. He began writhing in outrage, his ear-shattering shrieks reaching new heights.

"Please...please stop crying," Maddie implored. "I can't think. What am I going to do?"

She began pacing frantically in her hallway, holding the nearly apoplectic infant and wondering what she'd ever done to deserve this.

"Call the restaurant. That's the first thing," she mumbled. "Leave a message for Harrington that...that I'm having a little car trouble, but I'll be there as soon as I can. Okay. Then all I have to figure out is what to do with *you*." She stared down at the bundled-up baby, his crinkled face a bright scarlet as he took a gulp of air before breaking into new wails.

"Don't think I'm thrilled, either, kid," she said, blinking away some of her own tears.

Squealing babe in arms, Maddie headed for the kitchen phone but picked up a decidedly unpleasant scent as soon as she stepped into the room. An instant later her eyes fell on the smoking iron, and she let out a shriek to rival Timmy's. The iron that she'd thought was broken and had therefore set down mindlessly on top of her cognac wool dress had decided to function after all. "Oh, no. No. Why me?" she moaned, lifting the iron to reveal a large singed hole on the front panel of her dress.

The only good part was that Timmy seemed to find her newest predicament soothing. He stopped crying and stared up at her, a little smile on his face as he emitted a soft cooing sound.

"Oh, I see. A child who smiles at others' adversities." But Maddie's lips curved up faintly. "Okay, kid. Just keep it down until I make my call."

It was too much to ask. The minute Maddie got the maître d' at Simeoni's on the phone, Timmy began bellowing again. Maddie gave him the message but couldn't really hear the maître d's response with Timmy screeching in her ear. Of course, the instant she hung up, Timmy's squeals came to an abrupt stop.

"So that's the game you're going to play, is it? Do you have any idea how bad it's going to look for me to show up late for this meeting with Harrington? And now I not only have to find someone to look after you, I've got to dig up something else to wear, too. This has got to be one of the most impossible evenings of my life."

Timmy cooed.

Maddie sighed, using this moment of silence to ring Liz and hopefully enlist her aid. After a half-dozen rings, Maddie realized that Liz must have gone straight over to her sister-in-law's shower.

"Okay, think, Maddie. Think. Who else can you try?" She considered the occupants of the other five apartments in her brownstone building. She only knew them well enough to exchange pleasantries. How could she ask one of them to watch a strange baby?

After exhausting her list of friends, all of whom were either not at home or on their way out, she was desperate enough to ring up all of her neighbors.

Only one of them was home—Mrs. Johnston on the first floor. And she was just on her way out to visit her niece in Marblehead for the night. She did, however, offer Maddie a helpful suggestion. Mrs. Johnston's daughter sometimes used a baby-sitting service.

"Now let me think. Was it Wee Folks or Wee Love? Something like that. Oh, I remember. It was Wee Care. Isn't that cute?" Mrs. Johnston chuckled while Maddie forced a polite little laugh. "They have branches all over the area."

"Well, anyway," Mrs. Johnston went on, "there are quite a few of those services in the yellow pages. I believe they are all licensed and quite professional. You should be able to find a nice, capable person to look after your baby. Oh, that's right. It isn't your baby, is it? It's your nephew. No, no. Cousin. That's it. Well, good luck, my dear. Oh, that's my niece tooting outside. I must go. I'm sorry I couldn't be of more help. I do feel neighbors should help each other out. Now that we've gotten acquainted, you must stop in to have a cup of tea with me sometime."

Maddie was thumbing through the yellow pages before she even hung up the phone. It turned out that there were seven child-care services listed in the Boston area. The Wee Care Agency was the last one on the list. Crossing her fingers Maddie started there.

MICHAEL HARRINGTON DROVE down Storrow Drive
with snow swirling in front of his windshield. The
temperature was dropping rapidly, and the roads were
icing up. The cars in front of him were slipping and
sliding all over the place. Michael, on the other hand,
maneuvered his Lamborghini expertly, the sleek sports
car gripping the road solidly. He'd driven the car from
New York to Boston, leaving it parked in his mother's
driveway for a week while he flew down to Palm Beach.
Despite sitting idle all that time in the cold weather, the
engine purred like a contented tiger. He patted the
steering wheel affectionately as he pulled off the Government Center exit.

A young man in a blue parka with a Simeoni's em-
blem on the breast pocket darted out of the restaurant
with an umbrella as Michael drove up. Stepping out of
the car, Michael waved away the umbrella. The young
man closed it, tossed it over by the curb and gave the
Lamborghini an appreciative smile before driving it off
to the parking lot.

Another man, this one middle-aged and dressed in
formal livery, opened the large brass-and-glass door for
Michael, greeting him by name. A pretty brunette stood
behind the counter of the coat checkroom and beamed
as Michael approached.

"It's nice to see you again, Mr. Harrington. It's been
a long time." She gave him the same kind of appreciative smile the young man outside had given his sports
car.

"It has been a while." He smiled back, slipping off his
Italian black cashmere coat.

"Where'd you get that divine tan?" she asked, surveying a broad, angular bronzed face that wasn't so
much handsome as imposing, with its wide, square jaw,

slightly hooked nose and dark brows and lashes that framed eyes the color of midnight blue. It was his eyes that held her. Those midnight-blue eyes were capable of making a woman believe she was the only person on earth.

"I had some business in Palm Beach this past week." He smoothed back his thick hair, damp from the snow, with careless fingers.

"Mmm. Lucky guy."

The corners of his mouth lifted in a slightly tired smile. That Palm Beach trip had been exhausting—a week spent discussing, evaluating and surveying the L'Amour Skin-Care Company, one of two he'd narrowed his choice down to for the Barrett's special new line. He'd left Palm Beach convinced he'd found the right company. Which made his meeting tonight with Madeline Sargent of Sargent Skin-Care Products rather superfluous. Only a sense of fair play and the knowledge that the Sargent woman had gone to a lot of trouble sending him a detailed portfolio on the company made him decide to keep the engagement. He wasn't looking forward to having to tell her that he'd already made his selection. But those were the breaks. The least he figured he could do was treat her to a great dinner first.

"Ah, Mr. Harrington. It's good to see you." The maître d' greeted him warmly.

"Good to see you, too, Charles. How's the family?"

"They're fine. My son just got accepted at Annapolis. My daughter, on the other hand . . . well, she's a teenager. What can I say? My wife says most teenagers go through a stage."

"Tell me about it," Michael replied. "With six younger brothers and sisters I've seen every variation on that stage you could imagine."

The two men shared compatriotic smiles.

"Shall I show you to your table, or would you prefer stopping at the bar first? Your guest, Miss Sargent, telephoned to say she would be delayed because of some car trouble."

Michael rubbed his jaw thoughtfully. He could telephone her and suggest they postpone the dinner. He'd much prefer to cancel it altogether, but he never conducted business that way. He finally opted for the bar. He'd give her a few minutes to get here. Better to resolve everything now.

"Looks like a bad storm moving in off the coast," the bartender said, setting a bourbon and soda down in front of Michael.

"It's coming down pretty heavily already," Michael commented. "The roads are slick."

He nursed his drink for a few minutes and then decided to give Maddie Sargent a call after all. If she was still in, he'd offer to pick her up. His efficient secretary had noted the woman's home number and address in his appointment book. He checked it and then dialed a couple of times, but the line was busy. He finished his drink, left a tip and stopped on his way out to tell Charles he was going to see if he could catch Miss Sargent at home and give her a lift. If she'd already left, he would meet her back at the restaurant. "Unless," Harrington added, "I get stuck out there."

MADDIE WAS GROWING increasingly frantic. Wee Care was all booked up. So was the TLC Agency, Baby's Best, Mary Poppins, Les Petits and Goosey Gander.

Maddie had one last hope—Hugs Plus. She'd already tried them a couple of times, but their line was busy. This time she finally got a ring, only to be put on hold with a medley of Muzak lullabies.

Crossing her fingers, she sat on the couch, Timmy squirming, but quiet, on her lap. Once it had dawned on her that the poor kid was probably boiling under all the layers of clothes Linda had put on him, she'd managed to strip him down to his terry playsuit. He'd rewarded her with blissful silence.

Maddie was considering this momentary good fortune when she felt her lap grow decidedly damp. Of course she'd already thrown on that little black number Liz had suggested earlier, deciding that the faint stain from the punch wasn't really noticeable. This stain was not only going to be visible but was also going to make her smell about as aromatic as a skunk.

While Maddie muttered some very unmaternal words under her breath, Timmy cooed happily.

"Good evening. Hugs Plus. Can I help you?"

"I hope so," Maddie said with such a note of desperation in her voice that the woman on the other end of the line laughed softly. "I need a sitter. Right away. It's really crucial. Just for a couple of hours."

"Right away?" The woman paused. "Saturday nights are always so busy. I do believe all of our people are booked, but let me check for you. Perhaps due to the **storm someone has canceled. Can you hold a minute?**"

"Yes, but please, please try to find someone for me."

As soon as she was put back on hold, Timmy began to cry again. Maddie put the phone next to his ear. Maybe he'd like the canned rendition of "Rock-a-bye-baby" better than she did. He didn't. "Well—" she sighed wearily "—at least you have good taste in music."

The compliment didn't help any more than the Muzak.

"Come on, Timmy. Give me a break. With any luck, a nice Hugs Plus nanny will zip over here and rescue us both from torment."

She lifted the soaked child gingerly in her arms, clutching the receiver between her chin and her shoulder. "I know you need your diaper changed. As soon as I finish this call, I'll see what I can do. Don't expect much, though. I've never changed a diaper in my life. And to tell you the truth, it isn't one of those must-do things I had on my list of life goals."

Her words offered little solace. Timmy cried louder until he discovered her silver necklace. Fascinated, he stopped crying a moment before the Muzak clicked off. Maddie waited with bated breath.

"You're in luck. We do have a cancellation. One of our best young men is available. You don't mind a male nanny, do you? He's exceptional. Now some of our clients prefer—"

"No, no, that's fine. Wonderful," Maddie interrupted hurriedly, giving her name and address. "How soon can he get here?"

"Well, the weather is getting worse. But he doesn't live that far from you. He should be able to be there within fifteen minutes or so. I just need a little information first."

Maddie gave her Timmy's name, said that, as she recalled, he was about six months old . . . and yes, he was in great health. Judging from his fine pair of lungs, anyway.

"That should do it. You will leave our sitter your location and phone number, one other person to phone in an emergency, Timmy's physician's name—"

"Yes, I'll leave whatever information I can."

"That should do it, then."

"Oh, thank you. I can't tell you how much I appreciate it."

"We hope you'll become a regular customer."

Maddie smiled dryly. Not in a million years.

As soon as she hung up the phone, she scooped Timmy up from her lap, dug through the overnight case and pulled out a cloth diaper.

"Oh, great. Doesn't your mother believe in those nifty little disposable ones that they're always advertising on TV?" She stared morosely at the large rectangular strip of cloth. "Well, like I said, kid, don't expect any miracles."

She laid him down on the couch, realizing too late that she should have placed something absorbent under him. Gritting her teeth, she hastily set about her task. Timmy didn't make it easy, but she finally managed to remove his wet playsuit and the soaked diaper.

Timmy cooed. He also chose just that moment to relieve himself once more. Maddie screamed, leaping back. Timmy seemed to find her reaction positively amusing.

"Did your mother mention that you have a demented sense of humor, kid? But I'll get even with you," Maddie muttered as she hastily and haphazardly folded and pinned the new diaper on him. "Eighteen or so years from now you're going to be sitting at some family function with your girlfriend, trying to look cool, and I'm going to tell her just what you did to me, you little imp. Go on and laugh now if you want."

Which Timmy did until Maddie set him down on her rug so that she could quickly change her clothes—again. She pulled out a much worn print challis dress from the closet and glanced at Timmy. "What do you think, kid?"

Timmy burped.

"Yeah, well, it's clean and dry. That counts for something."

Not for much, according to Timmy. As soon as she slipped the dress on, he once again started exercising his vocal cords vociferously.

"Hey, what are you—a connoisseur of high fashion?"

When her doorbell rang twenty minutes later, Maddie had her coat on, her car keys in her hand and was wearing out her hall carpet pacing frantically with the howling infant. Timmy, par for the course, once again had a damp bottom, but she'd leave the next diaper change to a professional.

At the first ring she darted to the door and flung it open, practically throwing Timmy into the arms of the man standing there.

"Oh, thank God. I thought you'd never get here." She was out the door, talking fast as she raced down the hall to the still-open elevator. "His stuff is on the living-room couch," she called out. "My number's there, too. I won't be late."

"Hey, wait. Hold on a second—"

She was already in the elevator. "I can't. I'm late."

The man dashed down the hall with the screaming infant, but the elevator doors swished closed before he got there.

MADDIE ARRIVED AT SIMEONI'S thirty-five minutes late with a pounding headache and frozen toes, her car heater having chosen this opportune time to conk out. The Fates not only seemed to be against her, but they were also obviously conspiring to do her in.

Maddie's hazel eyes glinted with determination. It was going to take more than a wardrobe of ruined dresses, a recalcitrant iron, a malfunctioning heater and even a hysterical, uncontrollable infant to defeat her. At least that's what she told herself as she handed her coat over to the brunette in the coat checkroom.

She smoothed down her hair, which she wore in a neat, stylish blunt cut to her shoulders; then she took a deep breath to steady herself and proceeded to the maître d's station.

"I'm Maddie Sargent, Mr. Harrington's guest."

The maître d' looked over her shoulder. "Is Mr. Harrington with you?"

Maddie shrugged. "No. Isn't he here yet?"

The man picked up a couple of menus. "He should be back shortly. Shall I show you to your table, or would you prefer to wait in the bar?"

"The table, please."

He smiled pleasantly and led the way through the candlelit main dining room. Maddie had never been here before, although she knew that the restaurant was considered one of the finest in Boston. She was, however, too keyed up to appreciate the elegant decor and the savory aromas wafting up from the well-spaced tables she passed. Right now the thought of eating dinner left her feeling slightly queasy.

As the maître d' pulled out a beautiful mahogany table so she could slide onto the plush gray banquette,

Maddie asked, "Did you say Mr. Harrington would be back shortly?"

"Yes, that's right."

"Oh," Maddie said, taking her seat, "then he was here earlier."

"Oh, yes. At a few minutes past eight," the maître d' said, smiling pleasantly as he slid the table back into place. "Would you care to order a cocktail while you wait?"

"You're sure he's coming back?" Maddie queried worriedly. "He did get my message?"

"Oh, yes, I gave it to him myself. Car trouble, correct?"

Maddie grimaced. "Right. Car trouble."

"Actually, Mr. Harrington went to see if he could offer you a ride here, but it seems your paths didn't cross."

"He left to pick me up?"

"Don't worry. He said he would return if he discovered you'd already left. Can I get you a cocktail while you're waiting? Or a glass of wine?"

"Wine," Maddie muttered absently, a most disturbing sensation creeping into the pit of her stomach. The man who'd shown up at her door to watch Timmy...he *had* shown up to watch Timmy, hadn't he? He *was* from Hugs Plus, wasn't he? Of course he was. He had to be. It couldn't have been . . .

"Excuse me, Miss Sargent. Will that be red wine or white? We have a very nice Chablis Premier Cru or—"

"What?" Her hazel eyes had lost their glint of determination. They were slightly glazed now.

No, she told herself. No, it was impossible. It couldn't have been Harrington's arms she'd dumped Timmy into. She tried to picture what the man had looked like. What he'd been wearing. But it had happened in a flash, and she'd been so preoccupied that the man was a complete blur.

"Would you prefer red or white wine, Miss Sargent?"

"Oh . . . white." But what if it had been Harrington? Hadn't everything else that could possibly have gone wrong tonight gone wrong? No, she repeated silently. Surely he would have said something. Wouldn't he? Then again, she *had* raced out of there.

Just sit tight, she told herself reassuringly. *Don't jump the gun.* It was just as likely that Harrington arrived at her apartment after she'd left and the sitter from Hugs Plus had told him that she'd already gone. Any minute now Harrington would come walking into the restaurant.

She sipped the chilled white wine slowly. Twenty minutes later the wine was gone and Maddie was growing increasingly edgy.

As she stared blankly at her empty glass a few minutes later, the maître d' came over. "I'm sorry, Miss Sargent. Mr. Harrington just telephoned. He asked me to offer his apologies. He tried to phone earlier, but the lines were down temporarily because of the storm. He will not be able to keep his dinner engagement after all." The maître d' paused. "He said to tell you he's been unexpectedly detained."

"Unexpectedly detained?"

"He might have gotten stuck on the road."

"Stuck . . . right."

IT TOOK MADDIE nearly an hour to get back home. More than a mile from her street her car stalled, and she couldn't start it again. She walked the remaining distance, a good five blocks, in what had now become a raging blizzard. Oblivious to the cold or any fear of frostbite, Maddie's mind was obsessed by a far more catastrophic worry. Namely that the man she'd so cavalierly taken for the sitter from Hugs Plus was none other than Michael Harrington. The man who held her future in his hands.

Her future . . . and a soaked, howling baby.

2

WHEN MADDIE OPENED the front door, she heard a soothing male voice coming from the kitchen.

"Okay, Scout. Dinner's just about set. Ready to chow down?"

Maddie quietly slipped off her coat and took off her boots. She stood in the foyer shivering. It took a minute for her circulation to return, her frozen fingers and toes burning as she began to warm up.

She took a few steps in her stockinged feet into the living room until she reached a spot where she had a direct view into the kitchen. She remained silent as she watched the tall, dark-haired man, his back to her, standing by the stove. Timmy was slung casually and contentedly over the man's broad right shoulder as he expertly tested a heated bottle of milk by shaking a few drops onto his wrist.

"Perfect," he announced in a deep baritone, cradling the baby in the crook of one arm. He laughed softly as Timmy reached out with his hands to help guide the bottle to his lips.

"When's the last time your mama fed you, Scout?" He walked over to the kitchen sink and, letting Timmy manage the bottle for a moment, turned on the taps. "I'll get a nice bath ready for you, and then you'll be set to sack out. And as soon as your mama gets back here, she can tuck you in."

The man's move to the sink put him in profile. A strong, rugged and attractive profile at that. As he looked down at Timmy, his tanned face creased in a smile, crinkled lines deepening about his eyes and the corners of his mouth. His shirtsleeves were rolled up above his elbows, the muscles in his forearms rippling as he moved.

When he shut off the taps and turned away from the sink, he spotted Maddie. He was startled for a moment but quickly composed himself.

"Where'd you learn how to diaper a baby? In a war zone?" The corners of his mouth twitched in a faint smile; his dark blue eyes held her transfixed.

Maddie stared at him for a long moment. And then she threw her head back and broke into a soft peel of laughter.

The man continued to regard her as he walked with the still-contented Timmy in his arms into the living room and waited for her to calm down.

"Care to share the joke?"

Maddie sank onto the soft cushions of her sofa. "I'm sorry," she said as soon as she got the laughter down to a giggle. "It's just . . . for a while back at the restaurant I thought I'd made the supreme mistake of my life."

"And what mistake is that?"

Maddie didn't answer immediately. Instead, she watched the man remove the nearly empty bottle from Timmy's mouth, swing the infant over his shoulder and rhythmically pat his back until Timmy let out a resounding burp.

"That's better, Scout. Now you can finish up your dinner." He swung the baby back into the crook of his arm again and stuck the bottle in his mouth. All this without a cry, a whimper of protest or even a scowl from Timmy.

"You're terrific," Maddie exclaimed, hastily adding, "with babies. You must have been at this line for some time."

The man smiled enigmatically. "I've had my share of experience." He surveyed her face closely, and then his gaze dropped for a moment to take in her long, shapely legs. "So tell me about the mistake you almost made."

Maddie uncrossed her legs, self-consciously pulling her dress down over her knees, and sat up straighter. She cast the man a demure glance only to find his smile tinged with amusement. Maddie was dismayed to feel herself blushing.

"It's just . . . well, for a minute or two back at the restaurant I thought I'd actually . . . left Timmy with the wrong man."

"The wrong man?"

"I was afraid that you weren't the male baby-sitter from Hugs Plus. That instead you were my dinner date who'd come to pick me up. Well, not exactly my date. I was meeting the man on business. I've never even set eyes on Michael Harrington. And since I'd never met either one of you . . . well, it was certainly possible that I'd made a walloping boo-boo. And then, when he called the restaurant and left a message for me that he'd been unexpectedly detained . . . I started to think . . . Well, that's one worry off my mind. Not that I don't have plenty enough to still worry about. I've probably messed up my big chance with Harrington by not showing up on time." Maddie sighed wearily, her gaze on Timmy, who was now asleep in the man's arms.

"Why is it," she pondered half to herself, "that the one time in my life I'm desperate for everything to go

right, nothing, absolutely nothing, does." She paused,
then managed a weak smile. "Except for you showing
up and calming Timmy down . . . and taking such good
care of him."

Her compliment seemed to disconcert him. Maddie
could even make out a telltale hint of redness rising
from his neck. His reaction surprised her. With his
looks, his build, his self-assured style, Maddie took him
to be the type to get lots of compliments from women
all the time. And the type who took them in his stride.
This unexpected show of vulnerability in him touched
her. And, in turn, left her feeling embarrassingly ado-
lescent. Could she actually be developing a schoolgirl
crush on her baby cousin's sitter?

"Well, anyway," she went on hastily, trying to dispel
the disturbing reaction she was having to him, "once I
walked in and saw you with Timmy. . . well, I was positively relieved to see my worst fears hadn't been realized after all. Michael Harrington certainly wouldn't
have been standing in the kitchen with an infant in his
arms, cooing to him, testing his milk, running his bath."
Maddie wished the sitter wouldn't keep studying her
with those incredible, hypnotic blue-black eyes. "So,
uh, do you do this kind of work . . . full-time?"

It was his turn to laugh. "No, not anymore. Truth is,
I'm out of practice."

"Oh. They told me at Hugs Plus that you were one
of their best."

"Hugs Plus said that, did they? One of their best?"

He was playing with her, she realized. And the game
was clearly seductive. Well, she'd have to put an end to
that right this minute. She stood up abruptly. "So how
much do I owe you? I never did ask about the rates." She
started across the room for her purse.

Timmy woke and began squirming. "Take it easy, Scout. Your mama's here. She'll give you your bath and tuck you in."

Maddie stopped in her tracks. "Oh, his bath." She turned slowly. "Look, since you're here anyway and were just about to bathe him when I came in . . . why don't you do it?"

He cocked his head. "Still a nervous new mom, huh?"

"I'm not a mom." She gave Timmy a rueful glance. "He's . . . on loan."

"On loan?"

Maddie's eyes narrowed. "My cousin arrived on my doorstep about a half hour before you did. She was in hysterics, begging me to look after Timmy while she raced off to Colorado to try to save her marriage. Her husband is having a hard time coping with being a father, and he's having serious second thoughts about the whole thing. Believe me, twenty minutes with this kid and I can see daddy's point. I've never taken care of a baby in my life. And that kid in your arms scares the living daylights out of me."

He grinned at her. "This kid? Hey, Timmy's a great kid." He walked over to Maddie. "You two must have just gotten off to a bad start."

Maddie laughed dryly. "You've got a gift for understatement."

"Come on. Take him in your arms and hold him."

Maddie backed off. "No...really. Every time I touch him, he starts to wail."

"I'm the pro, right? Go on. Take him. I'll give you a few pointers."

Maddie pressed her lips together and stared at the baby. She was sure Timmy was eyeing her as warily as she was eyeing him.

"Just relax. Babies can pick up all kinds of vibes. Just like adults can." He reached out and rested his free hand on her shoulder.

A tiny shiver went through Maddie at his touch. She pressed her lips together tighter.

"See. You're tense." He gently massaged the curved area where her neck and shoulder met.

His ministrations only made her tenser. "Okay, okay," she said, a tinge of desperation in her voice, "give me Timmy."

The minute the baby was in her arms, his face reddened and he broke into an outraged scream.

"See. See, I told you. He does this every time." She tried to return Timmy, but the sitter merely gripped her arm.

"Come on. We'll bathe him together." He had to bend very close to her ear to be heard.

His warm breath only served to agitate Maddie more, which in turn heightened Timmy's agitation. She gave the sitter a panicked look. He finally relented when they got to the kitchen and took the now-hysterical Timmy from her.

A couple of tosses in the air, a playful nuzzle on his belly, and Timmy was actually giggling.

"Dr. Jeckyll and Mr. Hyde," Maddie muttered sardonically.

"I guess I've just got the magic touch." He tested the water with his elbow. "Warm it up a little."

"Why not put him in the bathtub?"

Michael grinned. "He might get lost in it."

Maddie managed a begrudging smile. "He is kind of little." She started to turn on the tap.

"Whoa. Pull out the stopper first, or we'll all be having a bath." His hand was over hers. "I bet you could use a nice, hot bath yourself. Your hand's like ice."

"My car conked out about a mile from here. I had to walk the rest of the way home from the restaurant." His hand was still over hers, rubbing some warmth into it. His caress gave her a deep, unexpected sexual thrill.

Take your hand away, Maddie, she commanded herself. *This is crazy. Get a grip on yourself. You're just temporarily deranged. You don't want to do anything foolish. Anything you're bound to regret later.*

"Are you okay?"

Maddie nodded. She pulled her hand away, stuck it into the tepid water and pulled out the rubber stopper.

"Okay, that's enough." He caught her wrist, plunging both their hands back into the water again as he guided the stopper back over the drain. "You're trembling. You aren't that scared of bathing this tyke, are you?"

She continued to feel that sharp sexual tug. "I'm just . . . cold still."

"Maybe we ought to hold off on Timmy and look after you first."

She nervously turned on the tap.

"Please don't do this." Maddie had trouble getting her voice much above a whisper. "Don't...come on to me. I'll be perfectly straight with you. I've had a lousy night. And somewhere in this city Michael Harrington is, no doubt, also having a lousy night. Chances are he's holding me responsible for it. What I'm trying to say is...I think you'd better leave. I'll give Hugs Plus a call first thing tomorrow and tell them you were . . . great."

He stared at her, a sharp tug of conscience causing his throat to turn raw. "Maddie..." His voice was a note deeper.

She looked up at him, surprised and disoriented to hear him call her by her first name. She realized she couldn't even remember his name although the woman from Hugs Plus had given it to her. The disastrous events of the evening really had left her temporarily crazy.

"Maddie," he repeated soberly, no hint of seduction in his voice now. "There's something I'd better tell you."

She stared at him. "What is it?"

He saw that she was flushed, knew that she found him disturbingly attractive. Just as he knew he was equally attracted to her.

His brow beaded with sweat. He felt like a first-class heel, even though he hadn't been the one to start the ball rolling. Maddie had done that. But he'd played along. He had to take responsibility for carrying the ball as far as he had. It was that devilish streak in him. He could be an incorrigible tease if given half a chance. And Maddie had left herself wide open. Having taken advantage of her vulnerability made him feel even crummier.

He took a deep breath. "Maddie, I'm not a babysitter. The fact is, the sitter from Hugs Plus called five minutes after you flew out of here like you were running the fifty-yard dash. He said he couldn't make it, that someone in his family was sick. I tried to call the restaurant, but I couldn't get through. To tell you the truth, I was steaming there for a while. Getting an infant suddenly dumped in my lap wasn't exactly how I'd planned to spend my evening. I felt trapped, and believe me, that's not a feeling I cotton to. But I couldn't very well leave Timmy here alone. And I knew that once you got my message, you'd be home soon. There was nothing else to do but sit tight. It's a good thing Timmy here was such a good sport."

Maddie nodded inanely. The truth was slowly registering.

"Anyway, when you walked in and still mistook me for the sitter, I got this urge to teach you a little lesson. Without really meaning to I guess I let myself get a little carried away."

"You're Michael Harrington." She gave him such a look of abject despair that he felt like digging a hole for himself on the spot.

"I'm sorry. It was a rotten stunt to pull on you. But I thought Timmy was yours, that you were just some ditsy dame who couldn't get her act together and..." He watched her pretty hazel-green eyes narrow, hostility emanating from them like burning sparks.

"You aren't the least bit ditsy." His throat was dry. "Not ditsy at all."

Maddie took a step back, slowly shaking her head, her arms clutched across her chest as the whole charade came sharply into focus. "What you're saying is that you deliberately made a complete fool out of me." Her voice was quavering with rage. "And what's more, you had a grand old time doing it."

"Maddie..."

"Don't call me Maddie," she shot back. "Only my friends call me Maddie. And another thing..." She stopped abruptly, realizing that she was sounding off to the man who still held her future in his hands. Had she gone irrevocably insane? Was she really about to simply toss her future out the window because of foolish pride? Anyway, she reasoned, hadn't she done to

Michael Harrington exactly what Linda had done to her? He'd come out in a raging blizzard to pick her up and what did he get in exchange for his kindness? A bouncing baby boy. Could she really blame him for wanting to even the score a little?

Tears stung her eyes. "Oh, Lord, when is this nightmare going to end? Why are the Fates out to destroy me?" she moaned, crumpling into a kitchen chair and dropping her head onto her arms, which were folded on the table.

Michael walked over with Timmy still snug against his chest. He felt rotten. Not only did he feel like a heel for misleading her, but on top of that he was also going to have to tell her she was no longer in line for the Barrett's account. He knew he shouldn't prolong her agony. Get it all on the table and then bid a hasty, if guilty, retreat.

But he couldn't bring himself to do it, not now, not when the poor woman was already feeling so low, no small part thanks to him. How much could she handle in one night? And a small voice inside him asked how much he could handle. Maddie Sargent was proving to be far more than he'd bargained for. Maybe, he told himself, the best thing to do was put off any further bad news until he got back to New York, where he could have his secretary write her a nice, businesslike Dear John letter.

He put his hand lightly on her back and felt the muscles beneath her skin tighten at his touch. "Look, I don't blame you for feeling angry. Or upset. I don't blame you at all. Maybe I'd better just take off now and let you get some sleep. I'm sorry, Maddie."

Maddie didn't say a word. Nor did she look up.

Michael removed his hand and straightened. He felt at a complete loss. He stared down at Timmy, who had once again fallen asleep, his tiny body curled contentedly in the crook of his large arm. "You'll have to take him now," he said softly.

Maddie lifted her head so that only her eyes were visible. They held such a vulnerable, unprotected look that Michael felt an urge to take her in his arms. Instead, he stood there awkwardly.

"You're leaving?" She raised her head a little higher, her voice anxious.

He broke into a slow smile. "It's been a tough night for you. And I'm sorry to think I made it even tougher." He tried to sound sympathetic, but he was distracted by a quick flash of desire. Maddie Sargent was very appealing, and he found himself wishing he'd met her under altogether different circumstances. He made it a rule never to mix business and pleasure. Then again, he reminded himself, he wouldn't actually be doing business with Maddie. Not that that gave him a viable edge. Once she learned that he'd not only humiliated her but was turning her company down for the new skin-care line at Barrett's, as well, he seriously doubted he'd have much luck wooing the woman. Michael frowned, realizing that he was in a no-win situation, a rare place to find himself these days.

Maddie lifted her head fully and stared at Michael with a pleading expression. "But...but you can't leave. Not like this. Give me a break, Harrington. Your walking out now would just top off this nightmare. You've got to give me a second chance," she said with a melancholy smile.

She saw Michael step back, and her voice took on a frantic note. "Look, it's still early. We can have that meeting here. I have this whole great pitch to give you about the line we want to work on for Barrett's. It's a knockout. I don't think that portfolio I sent you gives you more than a hint of where my company is heading, how fantastic our products are."

She had to stop to catch her breath, but she continued to watch him closely. She was afraid she wasn't making any headway and quickly decided to switch tactics. "Besides, you promised to help me give Timmy his bath. You owe me, Harrington. You admitted yourself it was a dirty trick to pull on me. I didn't deserve it."

Michael's smile was tender. "No, you didn't deserve it." He squinted down at Timmy. "I guess he can skip his bath. Why don't you take him now that he's fast asleep and tuck him in?" He met her gaze levelly. "Then I guess we can talk for a little while. But, to be honest, I'm bushed. I really am out of practice with babies. They can wear you out sometimes."

"Believe me, I know." She watched anxiously as Michael carefully transferred the sleeping infant into her arms. She held her breath as Timmy squirmed for a moment and then sighed with relief when he nuzzled against her breast, still sound asleep.

Her relief lasted all of two steps. The moment Timmy started to cry, Maddie froze. "Oh, not again," she moaned.

Michael came up to her. "Just rock him a little."

"He's allergic to me, I swear. Or else he just plain hates me. Here, you take him," she said, thrusting Timmy back into Michael's arms.

Michael grinned as his hand moved under the baby's bottom to support him. "He's wet, that's all. He's just letting you know he wants his diaper changed."

"When do they learn to ask politely?" Maddie quipped. "And how come he isn't screeching in your arm? For you he coos about his wet diaper. For me he hollers bloody murder."

He kissed Timmy affectionately on the top of his head. "Like I said, babies are sensitive creatures."

And, Maddie recalled, he'd also said that he'd had a lot of experience with babies. Did that mean babies of his own? She frowned. Hadn't Liz told her Harrington was single? Did she mean single *now*? As in once married?

"Where do you want to put him?" Michael's voice broke into her ruminations.

"Put him? Oh, put him. Um, I guess in the spare bedroom. Wait, Linda left me some sort of crib for him." She went ahead of Michael into the living room. The little plaid canvas car bed was beside the couch. She picked it up by its metal handles.

When she turned back to Michael, he was already heading down the hall with Timmy.

"It's the second door on the left." She hurried after him, the car bed knocking against her calf and causing a major run in her last good pair of panty hose. Well, it was par for the course.

Michael entered the small, not entirely tidy room that served more as a home office than a spare bedroom for Maddie. She dropped the car bed on the floor and scurried about the room, picking up. "I'm afraid I wasn't expecting . . . company in here," Maddie said, flushing. She'd given up worrying about her cheeks reddening. It was out of her control.

Michael watched her with a glint of amusement in his eyes. And a feeling of empathy. She really was having a tough time of it.

"Relax, Maddie. I'm no Mr. Clean myself."

She was bending over, picking up a pile of papers on the floor near her cluttered rolltop desk. Michael couldn't help letting his gaze wander down her lovely rounded bottom to those slender, beautifully shaped calves and ankles. She rose quickly and whirled around to face him. He felt a little like a small boy who'd got his hand caught in the cookie jar.

But Maddie was oblivious to Michael Harrington's intimate survey. "Oh, believe me, the room is clean. It's spotless. Just messy. I have a regular cleaning service. It's just . . . I do a lot of work in here." She ran her fingers nervously through her honey-blond hair, caught for a moment between anxiety and distraction as she finally took in Michael's warm, enticing smile. She stared at him. He was at least six feet two, and her fingers just itched to smooth his thick, dark, ruffled hair. He had the darkest blue eyes she'd ever seen, eyes that Maddie thought capable of being hard and cold, but which also could, like now, look heart melting.

Michael was the one to pull his gaze away first. He only managed it with difficulty. He set Timmy down on the narrow spare bed, but not before he slipped a magazine under the baby's wet bottom. "We're going to need another diaper." He could see Maddie out of the corner of his eye. She didn't make a move. "A new diaper," he repeated.

Maddie pulled herself together. "Right. Diaper." She hurried out of the room, returning a moment later waving the diaper like a white flag in one hand, the tote filled with the rest of Timmy's belongings in the other. "I thought everyone used disposable diapers these days. Now those make some sense. Or at least it looks that way on TV commercials." She walked up to Michael.

He'd already removed Timmy's diaper but was wisely holding it on top of him to avoid the kind of accident Maddie had earlier learned about the hard way.

She laughed softly, handing Michael the clean diaper. "I really am impressed. You are a pro. Is that because you have some kids of your own?"

"Me? Are you kidding? That's a definite no. And I have absolutely no plans in that area." He said it so emphatically that Maddie laughed.

"I see we have that in common, anyway. But I'm baffled. How come you're so great with babies?" And then before Michael could respond, she said, "Oh, all those brothers and sisters of yours."

Michael was smiling again. "I see you've been doing some research."

She flushed, but then she smiled back. "Okay, I know that you're thirty-four, you didn't make it to where you are by resting on any university laurels, you have six brothers and sisters, and you grew up in the South End." She took a breath. "What do you know about me, Mr. Harrington?"

His smile was sensual, generous, all male. It warmed Maddie to her bones. "I know I'd prefer if you called me Michael."

There was an awkward silence. Both of them were disconcerted by how easily they could slip into a relationship that was more intimate and complex than either of them wanted under the circumstances. Maddie had a rule that matched Michael's about separating her professional and private life. She also prided herself on never becoming too emotionally attached to any man. Raised by a divorced and fiercely independent mother whose work as an artist's rep kept her on the road a great deal, Maddie had learned at a young age to look after her own needs. She had grown into a self-assured, self-contained young woman. So why, she wondered despairingly, was she feeling so utterly inept and nervous since setting eyes on the sublimely appealing Mr. Harrington?

The tension Maddie and Michael were feeling got to Timmy, as well. Or else he was getting impatient to have his needs attended to. He broke into a loud wail and began wildly flailing his arms and legs.

Michael was relieved to have something less complicated to focus on. He pulled his key ring from his trousers pocket and jangled it above Timmy's face. Timmy's crying stopped midtear.

"I'd better teach you how to change a diaper. Tomorrow you're on your own." He could feel the tightness in his throat, hear the hint of gruffness in his tone. All at once he was feeling claustrophobic, panicky. Maddie Sargent was setting off too many sparks. Sparks, nothing. High-voltage charges.

He concentrated on the diaper, folding it diagonally and slipping it under Timmy's bottom. "It's perfectly simple. Just bring up the bottom flap," he muttered, safety pins stuck in one corner of his mouth, "grab the two ends on one side, pull, pin . . . be sure to keep your fingers behind the cloth as you stick the pin in . . . you'll cry a lot less than Timmy here if you get stuck . . . then the other side and . . . voilà." He lifted the baby and held him in his outstretched arms for Maddie's inspection. "Got it?"

Maddie grinned. "I doubt it."

"You will with practice." He rummaged through the baby's tote for a terry sleeper. "You want to try putting this on?" He held up the tiny stretch suit.

Maddie laughed. "I don't think it would fit."

Michael laughed back, his gaze instinctively trailing down her shapely body, the simple shirtwaist dress in no way inhibiting his vivid imagination. And in no way curbing his rapidly escalating pulse rate.

Their eyes met and then they each glanced away. Michael busily attended to Timmy, adeptly dressing him in the stretch suit.

"There," he said, straightening and clearing his throat. "You can have the fun part of tucking him in."

Maddie looked doubtful, but she gingerly held out her arms as Michael handed Timmy over. When the baby didn't shriek, Maddie smiled cautiously. "Hey, will you look at this. Not bad. Okay, Scout," she murmured, unconsciously adopting Michael's nickname for the infant, "we've got this under control." Carefully she pivoted, her long, slender fingers encircling Timmy's little waist. She took a few steps toward the car bed and placed Timmy down in it as if he was a delicate bomb that would go off if there was one false move.

She hovered over the bed after she released him. "Which way? On his back like this, or on his stomach, his side?"

She sounded so earnest that Michael had to smile. "He looks pretty happy just the way he is."

Maddie straightened slowly. "Yes, he does, doesn't he? He is kind of cute." She laughed softly. "I remember my mother telling me that I always looked beautiful when I was asleep."

She turned to him as she spoke. Michael fixed her with his dark blue eyes. "You're beautiful when you're wide awake."

Maddie gave him a heart-crushing smile. But she didn't say anything.

Michael came over to her. She could feel her whole body change as he approached, a tightening of her muscles, an alteration in her breathing. But when he was within touching distance, he merely glanced down at Timmy, winked at him and then headed for the door. "Come on. Let's get out of here while the going's good."

Michael's suddenly brusque tone threw Maddie, and it took a couple of moments for her to regain her equilibrium.

When she stepped out of the room after Michael, she saw that he was heading straight down the hall, picking up his suit jacket and overcoat from the entryway bench.

"Where are you going?" she asked, running up to him. "I thought we were going to talk...business."

Go on, Michael, say it now. Tell her there is no business to discuss. Go ahead. Really make her day.

"The snow's coming down hard. I'd better get going before I get stuck. Look, I'll be in touch with you. This isn't a good time, anyway. And..."

An eruption of wails from down the hall made him stop talking. But not walking. He really had to get out of here.

"It's Timmy." There was a note of panic in Maddie's voice.

"Just give him a couple of minutes. He'll settle down." Michael's hand was on the doorknob.

"But what if he doesn't?"

He had the door open. "Have faith."

Maddie smiled ruefully. "Oh, yeah, sure. Look where it's gotten me so far tonight."

He glanced back over his shoulder at her. For one optimistic moment Maddie thought he was going to change his mind about leaving. She even heard what she took to be a capitulative sigh.

Instead, it turned out to be a sign of resignation. "Look, I'm sorry, Maddie. I'll be in touch."

Maddie watched the door close. She stared at if for a long moment. Then she turned and looked down the hall toward where Timmy was exercising his vocal cords full force.

"How could you do this to me, Michael?" she muttered as she folded her arms across her chest, hugging herself tightly. It was bad enough that he was deserting a sinking ship. But having to figure out how to cope with Timmy was only half her problem.

Maddie was far more perplexed about how she was going to cope with the disturbingly unsettling emotions Mr. Harrington set off in her. She could not remember ever being thrown so completely off guard by any man. But Michael Harrington, she was forced to admit, wasn't just any man. He was tantalizingly good-looking, he had an incredible body, he was shrewd, self-assured, impossibly sexy. He was even good with babies.

In short, Michael Harrington had a lot going for him.

Including, lest she forget, the opportunity for her to put Sargent Skin-Care Products on the map.

3

WHEN MADDIE'S DOORBELL RANG a few minutes later, she dashed down the hall, a bright smile on her face.

I knew he wouldn't just walk out on me, she told herself as she unlocked the door. *The man's got a heart.*

She was still smiling as she opened the door, but her smile faded quickly as she saw the scowl on Michael's face.

"My car's been towed." He shook the snow out of his dark hair and entered the foyer, his scowl deepening. "I didn't pay any attention to the Snow Tow Zone sign when I pulled in to pick you up because I was only going to be gone for a minute."

Maddie felt a sinking sensation in the pit of her stomach. She couldn't have done more tonight to ruin her chances of winning over Harrington if she'd intentionally set her mind to it.

"You wouldn't happen to ever have had your car towed from here and know which lot the police take the cars to?" Michael absently smoothed back his damp hair from his forehead.

Maddie shook her head. "Sorry. I have a parking spot behind the building."

"I need to use your phone." Michael's voice remained gruff.

"Fine. I'll go check on Timmy. There's a phone... well, you know where the phone is," she said stiffly.

Of course, Timmy who had miraculously stopped crying just after the doorbell had rung, immediately began fussing again when Maddie peeked in on him.

"Terrific," Maddie grumbled, lifting Timmy up to check his diaper and praying fervently that her cousin Linda's plane hadn't been able to take off in the storm after all and that she'd show up at any moment to rescue her.

"See if there's a pacifier in that tote," Michael called out. "That should work."

A look of intense annoyance flashed across her features. "You think you know everything there is to know about babies," she muttered under her breath, her sense of pride rising to the fore. "Timmy is my responsibility. I'll manage on my own just fine." She gave Timmy a determined look, but the baby clearly doubted her word.

Two minutes later she'd pulled every item out of the tote. There was nothing that resembled a pacifier. She did find a rattle, and she shook it over Timmy's red face as he lay shrieking in the car bed.

She wasn't aware that Michael was standing in the doorway until he spoke. "The line's busy. I'll bet half of Boston is calling in to the police to ask where their cars have been towed to."

Maddie's failed ministrations with Timmy had caused her to break out in a sweat. She wiped her damp brow and shook her hair back out of her eyes.

"I'm sorry about the car. I'll pay for the towing." She looked away from Michael and stared down at Timmy. "Maybe he's hungry again."

Michael hesitated for a moment and then unbuttoned his coat and walked over to her. "Here, let me show you something," he said, taking the rattle from her hand.

Maddie watched, chagrined, as he turned it over and stuck the specially designed handle against Timmy's mouth. Like magic, the baby's lips parted, and he began contentedly sucking on it.

"Oh," Maddie said dejectedly. "I didn't realize..."

Michael was struck by the despairing look in her shimmering hazel eyes and felt himself involuntarily tremble a little.

"You'll get the hang of it." He reached out and gently touched her cheek.

Her lips parted in a tremulous smile. "I guess so. Anyway, Linda's due back on Monday."

Michael's hand slid from her cheek to her golden hair. "Then it won't be so bad." The timbre of his voice lowered. His free hand moved up to the other side of her face. He saw the despairing look disappear from her features, but not the vulnerability.

Maddie stood there motionless, lost in Michael's midnight-blue eyes. She could feel herself melting at his touch, but she had no desire to move away. "I usually have...everything under control. I...I'm just...so new at this. I mean...babies." Her voice was raspy. And none too steady.

Michael felt his heart pound. He smoothed back her hair from both sides of her face. "You're doing okay." He could smell her perfume, a spicy floral scent that made him feel light-headed.

"I am?"

Slowly he nodded. In spite of all his honorable intentions, he drew her closer. Her lovely mouth promised all kinds of pleasures.

Maddie tried to grasp any last remnant of common sense. But there wasn't any to be found. Besides, her body wasn't paying attention. It was letting Michael Harrington fold her against his firm, strong frame. She tilted her head back.

He grazed her lips lightly, tentatively, unsure if he was testing something out about her or about himself.

That barest kiss made her feel woozy. She smiled crookedly up at him.

Something in Michael exploded. He found her lips again. This time there was nothing tentative in his kiss. It was reckless, dangerous, exciting.

The way she kissed him back openly revealed her desire. And her panic. She broke away breathlessly, feeling far more disheveled than she looked. She was about to give Michael a speech that was bound to sound ridiculously arch when, fortunately, she was saved by some shrieks from Timmy, who had misplaced his pacifier.

Maddie and Michael grabbed for the rattle at the same time. They both laughed nervously. Kissing Maddie had shaken Michael more than he'd realized. His hand was trembling. So, he saw, was hers.

He moved his hand away, letting Maddie put the pacifier handle back into Timmy's mouth. The baby shot them both a look that seemed to say, "Just don't forget I'm here, too." As if Maddie could!

"He sure is a handful," she said awkwardly. "Do you want to try again?"

Michael eyed her with speculative humor.

Maddie felt her cheeks blaze. "I mean . . . the phone. The precinct. Your car," she stammered in a flustered rush of confusion and embarrassment. Seeing Michael look equally shook-up made her relax a little, and she broke into a warm laugh. "What a night."

Michael grinned, relaxing a little, too. "Definitely a night to remember."

Her gaze locked with his. "Will you give me another chance?" And then, seeing his lips curve into a sensual smile, she hastily added, "I mean the chance to show you that I'm really a perfectly levelheaded business-woman with just the right product for Barrett's?"

Michael felt a stab of guilt. His potent attraction to Maddie had let him forget, at least temporarily, about that all-too-disturbing matter. "About the account, Maddie..."

She raised her hand. "Wait, we can talk business later." She glanced down at Timmy. "Let's tiptoe out of here, and maybe he'll go to sleep."

Michael nodded. "Good idea."

They left the room, Maddie closing the door very carefully behind her, praying Timmy would not break into an outraged cry at their departure. Or at Michael's departure, anyway.

"So far, so good," she whispered.

Her stomach gurgled as she and Michael walked down the hall, and it dawned on her that she never had gotten around to eating dinner. And then she realized that Michael hadn't eaten either. "Why don't I make us something to eat while you try to track down your car?"

She turned into the kitchen, Michael following her. "I figured I'd just grab a bite back at my hotel."

"You don't stay with your family when you're in town?"

"No. I'm big on privacy. If you grew up in a house like mine, full of a half-dozen noisy, intrusive little kids who got into everything, you'd understand."

Maddie smiled wistfully. "I was an only child. It was just me and my mother. And she was gone a lot. She had a friend who lived next door who'd come over and look after me. And then I went off to boarding school starting when I was twelve." She shrugged. "Actually, there wasn't much privacy there. I have a thing about that, too."

Michael gave the wall phone near the stove a fleeting glance and then he slipped off his coat. "I think it's going to be awhile before I track down my car. Something to eat sounds good."

"Steak?"

"I'll help."

Maddie smiled. "Oh, no. I want to prove to you I can do something right. I happen to broil a mean steak. And I'll show you my expert skill with a salad, too. I even have a bottle of white wine in the fridge."

Michael removed his jacket, casually folding it over the back of a kitchen chair. "You have to let me do something. I'll set the table."

"Okay. Silverware's in the top drawer next to the sink. Plates are in the cupboard next to the fridge."

Michael glanced over at the kitchen table. "Shall we eat in here?"

Maddie shrugged. "What about the living room? We could make a fire and eat at the coffee table, if that's all right with you. I never have gotten around to picking up a real dining-room table. The truth is, I don't entertain very much. I'm so busy with work. I keep a punishing schedule. But don't get me wrong. I love it."

"Eating by the fireside sounds perfect," Michael said softly. For some reason, which he didn't want to analyze, he was pleased that Maddie was too busy to do a lot of entertaining. And it confirmed a feeling he'd had during their kiss that while Maddie had a very definite passionate streak, it seemed to come as more of a surprise to her than it had to him.

He gathered the plates, silverware and a couple of wineglasses and took them into the living room. After setting them on the coffee table, he took on the task of starting a fire. As he watched the newspaper and kindling take, he realized he hadn't tried the police station again. He glanced out the window at the snow, then at the phone and shrugged. No harm in waiting until after dinner.

"Can I do anything else?" he called out.

Maddie appeared at the kitchen doorway. "Yes," she whispered sotto voce. "You can keep your voice down. Do you realize this is the first five minutes of lovely silence I've had all evening?" They grinned at each other.

After a moment's hesitation Michael walked over to her. He leaned very close, sending Maddie's heart immediately into an erratic gallop. "Can I do anything else?" he repeated, this time in a murmur, his warm breath against her ear vibrating clear through her.

Her eyes widened. She smiled tremulously. From behind her came a sizzling sound. And as she stared into Michael's mesmerizing eyes, trying to decide whether, for once in her life, to throw caution to the winds, she picked up the scent of something burning for the second time that night. "Oh, no," she shrieked, whipping around. "The steaks."

Racing to the stove, she jerked open the door, a blast of smoke hitting her in the face. "They're burnt."

Michael was behind her, catching hold of her hand as she went to pull out the broiler tray. "Watch it. You need a glove. Here, let me." He reached over her for the pot holder at the side of the stove and lifted out the charred steaks. "Forget it, Maddie. They don't look so bad. I like my meat well-done." He set the broiler tray on top of the stove and put down the pot holder.

Maddie stared at him. She had a hard smile on her face, but Michael knew she was close to tears. "You'd better run while you can," she said, looking away. "Trust me, the way my luck's gone tonight, anything could happen. You're treading on dangerous turf."

Michael surveyed her face, taking in her heightened coloring, her honey hair, her soft, wonderfully shaped mouth. Maddie exuded a combination of strength and beguiling innocence that both intrigued and challenged him. "I'm beginning to realize just how boringly uneventful my life's been these past few years."

Maddie found herself wanting to know every uneventful detail. In fact, she wanted to know everything she could about Michael Harrington.

He kissed her and a small, welcoming sigh escaped her lips. His tongue slipped between her teeth, warm and sensual, exploring her palate, the backs of her teeth. The sensation ignited her, and she captured his tongue with her own. He pulled her hard against him, and she could feel the heat of his body.

When they pulled apart, they were both a little unsteady. Maddie's breathing was shallow and irregular, her heart racing.

He took hold of her trembling hand, bringing it to his lips. He kissed each finger, then ran his tongue lightly over the tips.

Maddie shivered, her eyelids fluttering closed. "I'm not good at this, Michael. In fact, next to looking after babies..." She opened her eyes. "I'm very conventional. And pragmatic. Mostly, I'm an all-work, no-play type of gal." She stared as Michael continued his erotic ministrations on her hand. "I could count all of my mad, passionate flings on that one hand you're so fascinated by, and we could skip a finger or two without any problem."

His free hand pressed against her back, his fingers lightly massaging each small bone along her spine.

"Oh, that feels good." The words escaped her lips just before she snapped back to reality. "I think we'd better slow things down a little." He pulled her closer. "We'd better talk," she said with a gasp.

He frowned. The idea clearly didn't please him. Even though he knew she was right.

She took a steadying breath. "Look, Michael, I seem to have given you every wrong impression about me possible tonight. I so desperately wanted this evening to go off without a hitch. Instead, I've slammed into every hitch in the book. I'm on awfully shaky ground right now, and we haven't started negotiations. How about a rain check?" Some of the intensity left her face, and she gave him a wry smile. "A snow check might be more appropriate. What about Monday night? Linda will have collected Timmy, and I promise not to be the least bit . . . ditsy." She stared down at her hand, still securely clasped in Michael's.

He followed her gaze, reluctant to release his hold on her, although he had to agree that her suggestion made good sense. He was hoping to figure out a way to graciously turn her down for the Barrett's deal and not come out of it smelling like a skunk. He told himself he had no reason to feel guilty about selecting another company for the Barrett's line. He'd been leaning toward L'Amour even before he made that trip to Palm Beach. It was a larger, more established operation, and Barrett's had done business with them before. He blamed this whole sorry mess on his executive secretary, Ruth Arnow. If she hadn't raved about some new Sargent products she was using, Michael would never have contacted Maddie at all. But Ruth had made him curious. So he'd asked Maddie to send him some information on the company, and he'd set up this business date. Another mistake, this one his. He should have waited until after he'd talked with Helen Dennis of L'Amour. Well, it was too late now to even hedge on this thing with Maddie. He and Helen Dennis had already shaken hands on the deal.

He let go of Maddie's hand. "Okay. Monday night. Shall we try Simeoni's again?" He'd have another go at it. Wine her, dine her. And break the news gently. Like she'd said before, he owed her.

She grinned. "Don't you think we'd be tempting fate?"

He had to laugh. "I'm willing to take the risk if you are." His laughter faded as he was once again swept up in a desire to pull the appealing Maddie Sargent back into his arms.

It was Timmy's sudden, shrill cry piercing the silence that brought Michael to his senses. "You want me to settle him back down?"

Maddie took a quick breath, a determined glint lighting her beautiful hazel eyes. "Nope. It's about time Timmy and I came to a little understanding. You go ahead and call the police about your car."

Maddie's determination faded as she approached Timmy's crib a minute later. He seemed to have reached new heights of unbridled indignation. And the sight of her was anything but soothing.

"What is it with you and me, Scout? Why do we always seem to rub each other the wrong way? You want your pacifier again?" Maddie dug it up from the side of the thin mattress. "Here you go." But Timmy was in no mood to be pacified. "Okay, okay. Wrong guess. How about your diaper? Are you wet again?" She lifted him out of the bed. A strong pungent odor assailing her nostrils left no doubt that Timmy most definitely needed another diaper change.

Maddie gritted her teeth. Holding him gingerly in her arms, she retrieved a clean diaper and some premoistened towelettes from the tote. "Okay, Timmy. This is going to be a little tricky, but if you stop wailing, I'll give it my best shot."

While Maddie was in the bedroom steeling her nerves for yet another first, Michael was in the living room breathing a sigh of relief after finally getting through to the local precinct.

"Yes, Officer, a 1988 Lamborghini, New York plates, parked outside of 1349 Commonwealth Avenue. Yes, I realize the snow-removal trucks have to clear the streets. I only meant to be parked there for a couple of minutes. Could you just tell me what the fine is and where I can pick up my car?"

Before he got his reply, Maddie heard a loud "Oh, no" coming from down the hall.

"Michael, come quick." Maddie's voice sounded panicky.

"Just a sec, officer. I'll be right back. Don't . . . don't hang up, please," he pleaded to the cop on the line, knowing, before he got the words out, that the line would be dead when he returned.

"This better be good," he muttered, dashing down the hall into the spare bedroom. Maddie looked anxious as she stood by the bed watching over Timmy, whose tears had changed to rather frantic hiccups.

"Oh, Michael, something's the matter with Timmy."

"For heaven's sake, Maddie, it's just hiccups. The kid's been crying so much."

Maddie shook her head impatiently. "No, Michael. I'm not talking about the hiccups. This is serious. He's got a terrible rash."

Michael gave her a questioning look and walked over. He bent down to survey the plump, naked baby, who, while still hiccuping, looked up at Michael with an angelic smile.

"Well . . . what do you think?" Maddie asked.

Michael straightened, rubbing his jaw thoughtfully. "Malaria, possibly. Tell me, has this little guy been crawling around any jungles recently?"

Maddie stared at him, dumbfounded. "Jungles? What are . . ." She gave him a fiery look. "Michael, this is no time for jokes. I'm responsible for this baby, like it or not. When Linda brought him here, he looked perfectly healthy. And now look at him. He's covered with welts. It almost looks like he's been beaten."

"Maddie." He put his hands lightly on her shoulders. "You really don't know a blessed thing about babies, do you?"

"Until Timmy arrived on my doorstep, I could count on one hand the number of times I've even held a baby in my arms."

Michael grinned. "And you could even skip a couple of fingers, right?"

Maddie frowned. "You are an incorrigible tease. Please be serious, Michael. Do you know what's wrong with Timmy?"

He smiled softly. "Timmy's going to be fine, Maddie. All he's got is a bad case of diaper rash. Babies get it all the time. You should have seen my brother, Alan, when he was a baby. He had it the worst. Very sensitive skin. But all the kids got diaper rash on occasion. It's not anything to worry about."

"It looks so awful, though. And it must be painful."

Michael winked at Timmy, who, rather than bemoaning his condition, seemed quite pleased with all the attention he was getting. Michael reached down and tickled the baby's tummy, and Timmy squealed in delight.

"You're wonderful with babies," Maddie said, a touch of envy creeping into her voice. "You know how to make them laugh, how to soothe them, even what ails them."

An enigmatic look darkened Michael's features. "I really didn't learn about babies by choice. I was fourteen when my dad died, and my mom took a job working nights. My sister Kelly was six months old. Alan was a little over a year and a half. Jessie was going on three and stubbornly uninterested in toilet training. Between me and my mom we had our hands full. And there were no helpful next-door neighbors. No money to hire baby-sitters. I was it. While my mom was off doing the night shift at a local bank, I was the chief diaper changer, bottle washer, nose wiper and arbiter of scrapes between the older ones. I had enough experience looking after kids to last a lifetime."

He stopped abruptly, giving Maddie an awkward smile. "Sorry, I didn't mean to give you some hard-luck story."

There was an underlying sadness in Michael's voice and she wanted to urge him to tell her more about himself, about what it was like for him growing up, bearing those weighty burdens of responsibility. It had been so different for her. Unlike Michael, who had so many ties holding him, she'd had none. Her only responsibility growing up was simply not to be a burden to her mother in any way or to hamper her mother's freedom. For a fleeting moment she found herself envying all of Michael's brothers and sisters for having had this remarkable older brother to look after them.

Michael misread the intensity in her eyes. "Don't get me wrong. There were plenty of fun times, too. They're really a great bunch of kids, all the hassles notwithstanding. I just don't plan to create any new hassles, if you know what I mean."

Maddie grinned. "I know exactly what you mean." Her expression turned serious as she looked down at Timmy. "No wonder my mother flew the nest as soon as she could. Just look at me. I've had a baby for one evening, and I'm a complete wreck. I've always seen myself as a woman who could do anything well if I set my mind to it. I've started my own business from scratch, I've put in more twenty-hour days at the plant than I can count on your hands, mine and Timmy's combined; I'm twenty-eight and I head a loyal staff of over thirty people. . . ."

Her eyes misted slightly as her gaze continued to rest on Timmy. "Babies are so tiny, so vulnerable, so needy. I can't picture my mother coping with me when I was Timmy's age. My dad had already walked out on her by then. Felicity once told me he'd only stayed around to see her through the delivery and until she was on her feet again."

"That must have been tough."

"Felicity never really talked much about it."

Michael looked at her with compassion and tenderness. "Tough for you, too. Growing up without a father."

Maddie looked away. Her voice held an acid note. "I used to tell myself I couldn't very well miss someone I never knew. I never saw my father when I was a kid. He wrote me a few letters, but I never answered them. I hated him for deserting me. And later, when some of that hate gave way more to hurt, I thought it would be disloyal to Felicity to have any contact with him."

Absently she stroked the soft fuzz on Timmy's head. He smiled up at her, but her eyes, while fixed on him, were looking into the past. "Felicity isn't exactly the maternal type. I guess that's why I've called her by her first name rather than Mom since I was a teenager. She always seemed so awkward and uncomfortable when she had to play the role of mother. Not that I was all that great at playing the role of daughter. Neither of us ever really knew how to act with each other."

"Maybe you both were trying too hard," Michael said softly.

Maddie stared at him, a curious expression on her face. "I always thought it was because we didn't try hard enough. We didn't have much practice. We really didn't see each other all that much. Her work took her all over the world. Oh, I spent time with her during my school vacations and summers, but most of the time she was traveling, and I just got dragged along. She still travels a lot."

"What kind of work does she do?"

"She's a very successful artist's rep. Commercial art, mainly. And she acts as liaison between artists and big corporations. That kind of thing. It was exciting to go around with her once I was old enough not to be left in the care of one or another of mother's hired assistants. But still, we never really talked much. Not about anything personal. We still don't although we seem to have developed a reasonably comfortable relationship these days. She pops into town every few months, and we go on mad shopping sprees and eat ourselves sick in some of Boston's best restaurants. We really have a great time."

"Sounds like fun," Michael said, but there was something in his voice that led Maddie to think he didn't quite buy her enthusiasm. She didn't buy it completely herself. There were still moments when she wished she'd had the kind of mother who kissed her children's scratched knees, made them special treats when they had colds, read stories to them at night, sang lullabies. But she wasn't a little girl anymore. Surely she didn't need a mother's kisses for her hurts.

Michael surveyed Maddie's face. She seemed to him like a finely cut gemstone, faceted with myriad emotions. For a man who had always prided himself on never getting too involved with any woman, he could feel the intensity of Maddie's emotions with a depth of feeling that startled him.

Maddie felt unbidden stirrings in her body as their eyes held. Out of a growing discomfort, she turned away and glanced back down at Timmy, who seemed quite content for the moment as he paused in his survey of his tiny fingers to look up at her.

"Michael," Maddie whispered excitedly, clasping his wrist, her eyes still on Timmy. "Look, he's smiling. At me. He's smiling at me. This is a first." She glanced up at Michael. "Or is it gas? I remember my friend Sue Gardner told me that—"

"He's smiling at you, Maddie." Michael's hand moved over hers. "He's got good taste. Knows a beautiful woman when he sees one."

They smiled at each other. Maddie felt a warm glow suffuse her. Never before had she been so instantly charmed and thrilled by a man. Never before had she felt so overwhelmed.

Overwhelmed enough to be glad for once to have Timmy here to focus on. "So what do we do about diaper rash, Papa?" she asked, avoiding Michael's steadily intimate gaze.

Michael's thoughts were far removed from cures for diaper rash. He was caught up in wondering just what he was going to do about Maddie Sargent. He knew the wise thing to do, but he wasn't feeling very wise at the moment. He was feeling very aroused. He wanted to feel her warm, graceful body melt against him again; he wanted to experience the multitudinous pleasures of her lips, her tongue. . . .

Maddie's voice broke into his torrid thoughts. "Come on, Michael. You're the expert. What are we going to do about Timmy?"

Michael reluctantly pulled his gaze away from Maddie and concentrated on the baby, who was now busily examining his toes and having a grand time doing it.

Michael grinned. "Timmy looks perfectly content. I think he likes lying around naked." His grin broadened. "I like it myself . . . on certain occasions."

Maddie had a most maddening vision of Michael sprawled on her bed, his tanned, naked body against her lily-white sheets. Against her lily-white body.

"But I suppose we should put something on that rash before we diaper him again," Michael was saying.

It took a moment for his words to register. Michael broke into a grin, his fingers finding their way to her hair. "You weren't listening. What were you thinking about?"

"I was listening. You said . . . put something on his rash. What do we put on it?" she muttered, trying very hard to dispel the vivid picture of her stunning naked Adonis and the flash of arousal both the vision and his touch had ignited.

"Let's see if your cousin tossed some medicated lotion in that tote." He slid the palm of his hand sinuously down Maddie's back before he reached over for the tote. They both dug their hands into the bag at the same time. Maddie withdrew hers first.

"No ointment," Michael said, smiling.

Maddie considered the problem for a moment. "I have an idea. Be right back."

A minute later she returned with a tube of her company's new hypo-allergenic treatment gel for dry skin. "We designed it for women, but there's nothing in the formula that could do him any harm."

Michael examined the tube. "Maybe it will help." He undid the cap. "I'll put the cream on his bottom. You can take care of the soiled diaper," he said, winking.

Maddie grimaced. "How about *I* do the anointing and you..." She caught his narrowed gaze. "No, I don't suppose that would be fair. I'm the volunteer mama, even if I didn't exactly volunteer." She eyed the folded diaper on the floor with dismay. "I don't know why Linda doesn't use those nifty disposable diapers. If it weren't snowing so hard, I'd traipse right down to the drugstore around the corner and buy some tonight. First thing tomorrow morning . . ."

"Go, Maddie. Take it to the bathroom and rinse it out."

"Right." Nose wrinkled, she lifted the soiled diaper from the floor and, holding it at arm's length, started for the door.

Michael laughed. "Ah, the joys of motherhood."

"I'll tell you one good thing about this whole experience," she said as she stopped to raise the window a crack. "It absolutely confirms my decision never to have one of my own."

"I agree wholeheartedly." There was a pause, and a slow smile settled across Michael's face. "They are awesome little creatures, though, aren't they?" He wriggled his fingers against Timmy's little hand, and the baby closed it tightly around two of Michael's fingers, his baby-blue eyes crinkling as he fixed on Michael and giggled with delight.

Before Maddie left the room, she looked back to see Michael doing another expert diapering job. Then he lifted Timmy in his arms and rubbed his back tenderly. Timmy cooed, settling his head in the spot where Michael's neck and shoulder met.

For a fleeting moment Maddie wondered what it would be like if Timmy were hers and Michael's. Then the pungent odor of his messy diaper cut sharply through the fantasy, and with a disgruntled sigh Maddie headed for the bathroom to cope with yet another first.

4

A HALF HOUR LATER Timmy was sound asleep, Maddie was dishing scrambled eggs out onto two plates in the kitchen and Michael was restoking the fire.

"Not quite steak," she said apologetically as she entered the living room.

"Eggs are fine." Michael was squatting in front of the fire. He pivoted to the coffee table and poured two glasses of wine. Maddie set the plates on the table and sat demurely on the couch.

Michael patted the carpet next to him. "Sit here. It's closer to the heat. You still look a little chilled."

But Maddie wasn't chilled at all. Quite the contrary—she felt uncomfortably warm. And nervous. Michael Harrington went very well with the decor. And he fit into her fantasies all too easily. Still, she rose and joined him on the floor, careful to leave a good two feet between them.

Michael smiled as he watched her settle beside him. "Better?"

Maddie popped a forkful of food into her mouth and nodded. She was on her second bite when she noticed Michael was watching her instead of eating.

"I thought you said eggs were fine. They're getting cold."

Michael smiled openly. He took a large bite. "Fantastic. Scrambled to perfection, Miss Sargent."

Maddie's brow creased. "Don't tease."

"It is a bad habit of mine," he admitted sheepishly. "I used to rib my siblings all the time. They always swore one day I'd get mine."

"And have you?" Maddie asked, raising one neat eyebrow.

Michael lifted his wineglass and took a sip. "I have a feeling my time is coming." His dark eyes sparkled as he gazed at her over the rim of the glass.

Maddie met his gaze for a moment, an amused smile on her face. But as they continued to stare at each other, her smile faded, and she grew increasingly uneasy. Michael Harrington, with his dark, mesmerizing eyes, had a way of looking at her that drummed at all her defenses. She chastised herself for allowing him to make her feel like a stricken schoolgirl.

She looked over at the fire, absently tucking her feet under her. The soft glow from the burning embers brought out red glints in her blond hair and made her flawless skin appear even more luminous, her hazel eyes almost amber.

Michael continued to watch her. Maddie was captivating. He wanted to tell her how lovely she looked, but instead, he drew his gaze away and focused on finishing his eggs. When he was done, he glanced over at Maddie's plate.

"Aren't you hungry?"

Maddie gave him a distracted look. "I was just thinking."

"About what?"

She looked at him wistfully. "Tell me about what it was like for you growing up, Michael. I . . . have this picture. . . ." She hesitated, laughing awkwardly. "Oh, you know. All those TV families where everyone squabbles, but deep down they're all very close. And there's always someone you can go to with your problems. Was it like that in your family, Michael?"

A soft smile tugged at the corners of his mouth. "I guess it was . . . sometimes. Especially before my father died. My dad and I were pretty close. He worked for the phone company as a linesman. He was a big, brawny guy with a gruff voice and a heart of gold. He was big on us toeing the line and keeping our noses clean."

"And did you keep your nose clean?" Maddie asked, thinking, even as she posed the question, that it wasn't very likely. Michael Harrington impressed her as having been a rough-and-tumble sort of boy.

He grinned. "I had my share of scrapes. And bloody noses. I'll never forget this one time when I was twelve, and I cut school and went down with a couple of buddies to an abandoned warehouse to smoke a cigar one of my pals had gotten his hands on. I was just getting my turn when who should arrive but my dad. Seems the school had called saying I hadn't shown up and wondering if I was sick. My dad took the call. He knew a bunch of us hung out at the warehouse."

"What did he do when he found you there?"

Michael laughed. "He tanned my hide when he got me home. A few well-placed smacks that hurt my pride more than my butt. The worst part was he made me and my three buddies finish that cigar before he dragged me home. I don't think I ever felt so sick to my stomach again in my life. It sure cured me of wanting to smoke after that. Which I'm sure was exactly what Dad had in mind."

Maddie smiled. "I think I would have liked your father."

Michael smiled back at her. "He was a good man." His smile faded as he looked into her eyes. "I still miss

him. He was the kind of guy... you never thought
would... die. He was so full of life. He seemed so strong,
so tough. I still remember the day it happened like it was
yesterday. I was sitting in freshman Spanish class when
a kid came in with a note for the teacher, Miss Alonzo.
She read it very slowly and then she looked up. She had
such a solemn expression on her face. I knew something bad had happened. I watched her gaze travel
down my row of seats. I was the next to the last kid in
that row. Tommy O'Shea sat behind me. And I remember thinking, poor Tommy. Something bad must
have happened at the O'Shea home." Michael shook his
head slowly.

"I'm sorry." Maddie looked at him with tears shin-
ing in her eyes.

Michael glanced over at her. He looked uncomfortable, as if he'd shared more about himself than he'd
meant to. "Say, do you like basketball?"

Maddie blinked away her tears, thrown by the
abrupt shift in the conversation.

"I have season seats. I used to go with my dad. I still
manage to catch a few games, and my brothers use
them a lot. They're big fans of the Celtics, too. I just
thought... maybe you'd like to go to a game sometime."

Maddie wasn't sure if he was offering her the pass or
asking her out on a date. She said vaguely, "That might
be nice... sometime."

There was a prolonged silence as they both stared
absently into the fire.

After a while Michael glanced at his watch. It was
nearly midnight. "Damn. I'd better track down my car."

Maddie rose, gathering the plates. "Go ahead and try
the police station again. I'll clear up."

Michael watched her for a moment. Then with a resigned shrug he got up and walked over to the phone.

It took several minutes to get through to the police station again. He was just writing down the information about where his car had been towed when Maddie looked in.

"Well?" she asked when he hung up.

He scowled. "It's over on Tremont near Government Center."

Maddie sighed. "If my car hadn't conked out on me, I'd drive you over. Which reminds me, I have to call my garage first thing in the morning and have them pick it up. Unless the police got to it first. I did manage to get the car over to the curb, but now that I think about it, I never even looked to see if I was leaving it in a no-parking zone. I was a little preoccupied with other problems at the time." Maddie grinned.

Michael, however, was not in a particularly cheerful mood as he stared morosely out the window. The snow was still coming down heavily. The idea of trekking across town didn't exactly thrill him. And he wasn't very optimistic about getting a cab, although he supposed he might as well try to ring up a few companies and see if he could get one to pick him up. "Any cab company you can recommend?"

Maddie shrugged and turned to stare out the window. "I think a dog-sled company might be a better bet."

Michael laughed dryly as he flipped open the yellow pages on the desk. Maddie returned to the kitchen to finish cleaning up.

She had just dried the last few dishes when Michael joined her.

"Any luck?" Maddie asked.

"Nope. Every cab company in town is tied up for hours." He picked up the forks and dried them.

They put the rest of the things away in silence.

"Nice and quiet in the place with Timmy finally settled down," Maddie said, slipping the last of the silverware into the drawer.

"Maybe that ointment of yours will do the trick, and Timmy will sleep through the night."

It was a perfect opening, and Maddie wasn't going to let it slip by. "We're working on a lot of new, exciting products now. I wrote you about that new skin toner we'd love to do for Barrett's. We've been doing a fragrance-free line, but for Barrett's I thought we'd come up with a product line with its own special scent. Something citrusy... kind of a cross between tangerine and lemon. It's unique, refreshing and different. And we've got a new moisturizing gel that you heat up and apply to puffy eyes and it miraculously chases away that fatigued look." She laughed and yawned at the same time. "I sound like a walking advertisement, don't I?"

Michael smiled uncomfortably as he fought back his own yawn. He'd conveniently put the whole business of the Barrett's contract, or more appropriately the lack thereof, on a back burner. But Maddie had reminded him that it was a pot with a strong potential to boil over and scald them both if he didn't attend to it. "Maddie... about the new line..."

Maddie yawned again and grinned. "I'm sorry. I guess I'm more exhausted than I thought. Look, Michael, I think the only sane solution to your problem is for you to stay the night. You can use the guest room," she quickly added. "I'll take Timmy into my room with me, and you can get a decent night's sleep. Tomorrow we can both cope with our errant cars. What do you say?"

Looking at her, smelling her floral fragrance, seeing the nervous set of those wonderful lips, Michael could feel the heat rise in his body. "I don't know, Maddie. I should go."

A whisper of a smile curved her lips. "If you're worried that you'll be bothered by Timmy waking you up...."

Michael laughed softly. Maddie'd hit on part of the problem, anyway. He was worried about being bothered, all right. But not because of a six-month-old baby. How did that old song go? "Bewitched, bothered and bewildered..."

Maddie's smile faded. She was certain he was laughing at her. "What is it? Are you afraid I'll panic again...like the diaper rash?"

He leaned forward a little, leveling his gaze on her eyes. "Aren't you afraid, Maddie?"

Maddie stared at him for several silent moments. "Oh." The word formed on her lips but was barely audible.

"Then again, there isn't a single listing for dog sleds in the yellow pages." He draped his arm lightly over Maddie's shoulder and steered her out of the kitchen. She came to an abrupt stop in the hallway, shifting her weight, uncomfortable with the sudden change in mood and with the seductive sensation of Michael's arm still around her shoulder. "I don't suppose we can just...start over again and forget what happened?"

"You don't mean only the comedy of errors, I presume."

She cast him a rueful smile. "You're not going to make this any easier for me, are you?"

He squeezed her shoulder and then released her, his expression tender. "Look, Maddie, I don't know about you, but I'm not likely to forget what it was like to kiss those warm, beautiful lips of yours. Nor am I likely to forget what it felt like to hold you in my arms. You're an incredibly appealing woman, Maddie. But I think we're both practical, sensible people. We just caught each other at a mutually vulnerable time back there. So . . . we lost our heads. Let's leave it at that."

Maddie straightened her shoulders. "I want you to know, Michael, that I don't lose my head very often." Her hand moved absently to her neck. "It's firmly secure now." Well, she was working at it, anyway, she thought, avoiding his gaze.

"Hey, so is mine." Without realizing it, Michael's hand moved to his neck, as well.

They looked at each other then, and both immediately dropped their hands to their sides.

Maddie grinned. "Now that we've cleared that up, I'll go move Timmy and you can get some sleep."

Michael caught hold of her wrist as she started to turn. "There's something else, Maddie. . . . Before I do stay the night, I feel I should make it clear that . . . well, that Sargent isn't the only company we're considering."

Maddie scowled. "Hold it, Michael. I don't want you to think for one instant that I'm trying to influence your decision because of my . . . my hospitality. It's a perfectly innocent invitation. And practical. I have a fantastic product line to offer Barrett's, Michael. Better than the competition. I don't need to use any other means to nab that contract. Staying here tonight in no way . . ."

Michael sighed. "Okay, okay. Let's just put business on hold for the night. What do you say?"

Her smile was tinged with relief. "Good idea." Her gaze drifted down to Michael's hand. His fingers were still wound around her narrow wrist.

He held on to her for another moment. Then he nodded faintly and released her.

"I'll carry Timmy into my bedroom, and then I'll come back and make up the guest bed."

"That's all right. Leave Timmy be. If you move him, you're likely to wake him up."

"But what if he . . ."

Michael grinned. "I'm a deep sleeper. If he squeals in the middle of the night, you can come get him and play mama."

"Play mama," she echoed, the notion making her grin. "Who would ever have thought . . ." Her voice trailed off as her eyes met Michael's. He was looking at her with a curious expression.

"And here I always thought that even devoted career gals secretly yearned to play that role . . . given half a chance."

Maddie laughed, but there was a hint of discomfort in the sound that she tried to ignore and that she hoped Michael would. "Well, this is one career gal who's never indulged that fantasy." She started down the hall to the linen closet. Michael followed her. "The only baby," she went on, pulling open the closet door and reaching for the bedding, "I'm interested in is my company. I've nursed it for a long time, and now I'm ready to see it take off and do me proud." She glanced at him as she piled a couple of pillows, a sheet and a blanket in his arms. "Sorry. We agreed not to talk business tonight. I just get carried away sometimes."

"But not too often," he couldn't resist saying, giving Maddie a broad grin.

She felt her cheeks redden, and she turned abruptly, fumbling with the towels, a precarious pile of them toppling to the floor. She muttered under her breath as she bent to pick them up. What was she doing? Gathering bedding for Michael Harrington had such an intimate feeling about it. Why hadn't she just let him go off into the night? He could have coped. He impressed her as a man who could cope with just about anything. He was certainly coping better with her foolishly offered invitation to spend the night than she was. She knew she wouldn't get a moment's sleep with Michael sleeping practically next door to her.

She stuffed the armful of towels haphazardly back on the shelf only to realize that she'd forgotten to keep one aside for Michael. She tugged one out, a couple of others falling to the floor. She gave them a firm kick into the bottom of the closet and slammed the door.

"There," she said tightly. "I'll just change your linens, and then we can both get some sleep."

"Maddie, relax." Michael shifted the pile of bedding under one large arm, his free hand lightly smoothing back her hair. "If you're having second thoughts, I could button up my overcoat, step out into that blinding blizzard and track down my car . . . or die trying, anyway."

She laughed. "Your siblings are right. You are an impossible tease."

"That's better." He plucked the towel from her hand and shoved it under his arm with the rest of his gear. "Okay. Now, I'll see to my bed, and you go get some sleep."

"You're sure you don't want me to help?"

"I'm a big boy, Maddie. Save the mothering for Timmy."

Maddie drew back with a little sigh. "Right. Sorry. I guess this mothering thing can be contagious if you're not careful. If I'm not careful." She walked backward a few steps as she spoke. "But I'm very careful. I'm not maternal by nature." She backed into the wall. "Well, I'll just go take my shower, and then you can have the bathroom." She hesitated for a moment and then started back down the hall. Stopping at the door to the bathroom, which separated the two bedrooms, she said, "If you need anything . . ."

Michael was at the guest-room door. "You don't happen to have an extra pair of men's pj's around."

"No . . . no, I don't."

He winked. "Glad to hear it."

With a half laugh she entered the bathroom. When she closed the door, she leaned against it and took a deep breath. She pressed her hand against her chest. Her heart was pounding. She could hear Michael shut his door. She could imagine him crossing the room, unbuttoning his shirt, moving to the very bed that had been hers before she'd splurged a few months ago on a new queen-size bed for her room.

She swallowed as she imagined hearing the thud of shoes. No, he'd taken his shoes off much earlier. They were in the front hall. *This is ridiculous*, she chastised herself.

She crossed her arms over her upper body, hugging herself, telling herself that she was overreacting, reminding herself that Michael Harrington was a potential business colleague. Okay, so he was a gorgeous, sexy, charming potential business colleague. Okay, so his kisses were inspired. Some men had talent. Michael was obviously one of them.

Who was she kidding? She couldn't remember ever feeling such intense desire for any man, let alone one she hardly knew. With a weary sigh Maddie pushed herself away from the door and turned on the shower taps.

Michael could hear the shower going as he made up the bed. He started to picture Maddie slipping out of her dress. Her undergarments would be silk and lace. White against pale, smooth, flawless skin. He imagined away the layer of silk and lace, envisioning her slender, shapely body, her fine legs stepping into the shower. He imagined the spray falling over her rounded breasts, hardening the nipples. He could see her there in the steamy, misty water, her skin glistening. He could feel the heat rising.

Just then Timmy stirred, letting out two little coughs.

The sound shook Michael abruptly from his fantasy. He was disconcerted to feel a thin bead of sweat across his brow. And his heart was pounding. He hadn't had a fantasy that vivid since he was a teen.

He heard the shower stop and forced himself not to linger on a luscious, naked Maddie stepping out onto a bath mat, reaching for a towel....

He shrugged off his shirt and undid his trousers. What was the matter with him, anyway? She'd taken him by surprise. That was it. There was a heat and passion in Maddie that he hadn't expected. As well, there was a softness and sweetness about her.

He knew what his problem was. Like Maddie, he'd been so focused on his career lately that he hadn't given enough time or attention to his more basic needs.

Not that he thought it wise to pursue those needs with Maddie Sargent. Too much time with Maddie and he knew damn well he'd have trouble putting her out of his mind. And Michael Harrington was not a man who was about to let a woman—any woman—interfere with his concentration.

He folded his trousers over the desk chair, his car keys falling to the floor. He picked them up and set them on the desk, noticing, as he did, a rather provocative postcard lying there of a young, tanned, muscular fellow in a manly pinup pose. Michael went to reach for it, shook his head and peeled off his socks. He started to walk away from the desk, but then curiosity as to who would send Maddie a card like that got the better of him.

On the back was a brief note in flamboyant handwriting.

Darling,
Tell me this man isn't delicious. Greece is simply swarming with them....

Timmy started to cry. "Okay, okay. Settle down, Scout," Michael muttered, walking over to the baby and rubbing his back as he finished the note.

Next time you must tear yourself away from that sweatshop of yours and join me. Who knows? You might find the love of your life.

Viva l'amour,
Felicity

Michael grinned down at Timmy. "Mothers. They're all the same. They all want their children to find themselves a nice—"

There was a light rap on the door. Without thinking, Michael called out, "Yeah?"

Maddie took the "Yeah" for permission to open the door.

"Oh," she gasped as she stood at the open door, her eyes sweeping down Michael's body, naked save for a skimpy pair of navy-blue bikini shorts.

Michael gasped "Oh," at the same time, but he was so concerned about having been caught red-handed holding a piece of Maddie's mail that for a moment he didn't realize it wasn't the postcard she was staring at.

"Oh," he said again, feeling doubly exposed once the light dawned.

"I . . . I heard Timmy start to . . . fuss." Maddie made an effort to look past Michael, but her gaze kept straying. "I was just going to take him into my room."

Michael shoved the card behind his back. "He's okay. He's quieting down."

"I . . . I didn't mean to . . . walk in on you . . . like this."

Michael grinned. "It's okay."

"Well . . . I'll leave Timmy, then."

"Okay."

"Okay, then."

"Good night, Maddie."

She was halfway out the door when she stopped, her back to Michael. "Given the way the rest of my night has gone, I guess I should have expected to finish it with a flourish." She glanced over her shoulder at the near-naked man who was smiling broadly. A smile curved the corners of Maddie's mouth. "Well, good night, Michael."

She was standing there in a plaid flannel robe that did little to flatter her figure, but that fantasy vision of Maddie in the shower flashed through Michael's mind.

For a moment a flood of heat overcame him, threatening to wipe out all sensible, rational thought. Only the soft, sweet vulnerability of her smile kept him from taking those few steps across the room and pulling her into his arms so that they could really finish the night with a flourish. Instead, he nodded, whispered, "Good night, Maddie. Sleep tight," and accepted the fact that visions of Maddie Sargent would drive him crazy for what little was left of the night.

5

LIKE A ROOSTER, Timmy was awake at dawn. It took a minute for Maddie to place the howling sound. Then, bleary-eyed, she began rummaging around for her slippers, gave up the search and struggled into her bathrobe as she hurried down the hall. She didn't care how sound a sleeper Michael Harrington was—Timmy's screeches could wake the dead.

Just as she knocked on the door, there was silence. And then Michael opened the door, a red-faced Timmy in his arms. Maddie's gaze dropped from Michael's bare chest, feeling a mixture of relief and disappointment as she saw that he had donned his trousers.

Timmy continued howling and began tugging on his ears.

"Is it his diaper rash?" she asked sleepily.

"Not a sign of redness there. That ointment of yours must be a regular wonder cream. He's probably just hungry."

"I'll feed him." She hesitated as she reached for Timmy.

Michael didn't release him. "I'm up, anyway." Their gazes met and held for a moment. A faint flush showed on Maddie's throat. She thought she must look a mess, her blond hair going every which way, no makeup, her eyes no doubt red from so little sleep. In contrast, she was struck by how good Michael looked, his dark hair tousled, a sleepy, sensual smile on his lips, his eyes...she had never seen eyes quite like Michael's. They had such extraordinary depth and feeling. His eyes were a mirror to his soul, she thought.

Michael's smile deepened. He wasn't the least bit put off by Maddie's wild honey-blond locks, her lack of makeup. He thought her skin luminous, almost velvety. It was the kind of skin that demanded caressing. He wanted to slide the palm of his hand along her warm, flushed cheek. He thought he knew where that touch would lead, and he wisely clutched Timmy with both hands.

"I'm sorry that you got so little sleep," Maddie said. There was a thickness to her voice, a quaver. "I should have taken Timmy into my room last night."

They walked together down the hall to the kitchen. "I always get up early," Michael said. "I like to put in a couple of hours of work before I get to the office. And...I don't know...since I was a kid, I always felt there was something kind of magical about dawn, the coming of a new day."

Maddie took the milk from the fridge and poured some of it into a saucepan to heat up. Then she poured some of the powdered baby cereal Linda had left for Timmy into a bowl. She smiled at Michael. "I wouldn't have guessed you to be a romantic."

"I don't give in to it very often," Michael said, a definite edge to his voice.

Maddie busied herself rinsing out a bottle. "I know what you mean," she muttered. "I guess when you're married to your work, like we are, there isn't much time for anything but blood, sweat and tears."

Michael laughed softly. "Old man Barrett has certainly extracted plenty of all three from me over the years. But it's been worth it. And the real payoff is yet to come."

Maddie lowered the heat under the saucepan and turned to Michael. "What's the payoff?"

"Jason Barrett is sixty-eight years old. He has no children. His only son died seven years ago. He plans to retire when he turns seventy. And he intends to pick one of his VPs to step into his shoes." Michael's dark blue eyes glinted with anticipation. "I'm the man to fill those shoes, Maddie. I've lived and breathed that company since I was fourteen. I know every nook and cranny of the business. And now, as VP in charge of creative marketing, I've expanded the scope of the operation beyond any of old man Barrett's dreams."

"Has he given you some indication that he intends to hand the reins over to you?" Maddie asked.

Michael's laugh was caustic. "You'd have to know Barrett to realize the folly of such a question. The old man gives nothing away. He's tightfisted, tough-minded, and he likes to keep his people guessing. It keeps us all on our toes. Barrett will play the waiting game with us right to the bitter end. But I'm as close to the old guy as they come. He took me under his wing way back when I was just starting out there. He thought I had the right combination of guts and ambition. He made me a department manager when I turned twenty. I was the youngest staff person put into a managerial position. And I'm the youngest vice president in the company now. Barrett has let me know all along that if I kept playing hardball, I could make it to the top. We've each kept our end of the deal so far. Barrett's a tough nut, but he's a straight shooter. I'm pretty fond of him. In a way, he's been a kind of father figure for me over the years."

Maddie set the bowl of cereal on the table, tilted her head and contemplated him. "I bet you'll make it to the top."

"Thanks for the vote of confidence. As long as I keep my wits about me and follow through on my strategic plans for the next two years, you just may be right."

Michael held Timmy in his lap while Maddie fed him the cereal. He couldn't help feeling touched by the warm, cozy scene—Maddie, in her flannel robe feeding the baby, the faint rays of sunlight filtering into the kitchen, the lingering scent of last night's fire, the muted sounds of snowplows outside.

"Shall I give him his bottle now?" Maddie asked after Timmy gobbled down the last spoonful of mush.

"In the living room. It's more comfortable."

Michael settled Timmy in Maddie's arms and sat down beside her on the velvety wine-colored couch as Timmy greedily drank his milk. Maddie smiled, then let her head lean back on the cushions. Michael put his arm around her to make her more comfortable. She stiffened for a moment and then let herself relax against him. She watched Timmy devour his milk, unaware of the warm smile of pleasure on her lips. She turned her head to look at Michael. His eyes were on her, intimate and absorbed. Neither of them said a word. Maddie's lids fluttered closed. A few moments later, when she looked up at Michael again, he was asleep. She smiled, glanced down at Timmy, whose head had lolled away from the empty bottle and come to rest against her breast. He sighed with pleasure, found his thumb and closed his eyes.

With a sigh of contentment unlike any she could ever remember feeling, Maddie closed her eyes again, snuggled more comfortably against Michael and fell asleep, too.

Sunlight was streaming into the room when she woke with a start, but as she began to rise, Michael's grip on her shoulder stopped her.

"Take it easy. Do you always wake up in a panic?"

Only, she thought silently, *when I've fallen asleep nestled in the arms of a bare-chested, near stranger.*

"Timmy...where's Timmy?" she said in alarm looking down to her empty lap, afraid that in her sleep she'd somehow dropped him.

"I put him back in his crib. He's fast asleep."

"Why...didn't you wake me?" She didn't, however, ask why he'd come back to take her in his arms again on the couch.

"You're a pretty sound sleeper."

"Please. Let me sit up."

He obliged and Maddie sat up ramrod straight. "How do real mothers do it?" She yawned, rubbing her scratchy eyes, trying her best to return her tangled hair to a modicum of order.

Michael smiled. "It isn't easy. I was always amazed at my mother's ability to juggle all us kids, look after the house and put in a full eight hours' work at the bank."

"She was lucky to have a son who was willing to help her so much. I bet a lot of kids in your position wouldn't have been so selfless."

"Whoa." Michael laughed, embarrassed. "I was no saint, Maddie. I did what I had to do, that's all. After my dad died, there was no one else my mother could turn to for help. Believe me, I wasn't thrilled about having to give up—" he paused, his voice lowering "—a lot of dreams."

Maddie turned to him. "What kinds of dreams?"

Michael shrugged. "Oh . . . kids' dreams, dumb dreams. I made out just fine without them. I can't complain." His expression tightened faintly. "Like I said before, I paid my dues with blood, sweat and tears. And, for the record, I'm certainly not the least bit selfless. I look after my own needs very well, Maddie. There's not a thing I'd change about my life at this moment." There was an unmistakable look of defiance in his dark blue eyes.

His words hung in the air. Maddie rose, adjusted her robe, tightening the tie belt. "Ditto." And then there was a whisper of a smile. "Except, of course, seeing a Sargent line at every Barrett's department store across the nation." She saw the hooded look in his eyes and was annoyed with herself for pushing at the wrong time. With Michael negotiations had to be according to his timing, his plans, his lead. That irritated her, but Maddie was a smart enough businesswoman to realize the goal was too important to get into a battle of wills with Michael. Besides, she wasn't at all confident that she'd come out the winner. She was not misled by Michael's tender, even vulnerable side. The other part of him, she knew, was tough as nails, shrewd, determined and, perhaps like his mentor, old man Barrett, intent on keeping hold of the reins until the very end.

With a sigh of resignation Maddie said, "I'll put on some coffee."

"I'll go shower, then, and finish getting dressed." Michael's hand moved down the ripple of muscles on his bare chest as he spoke. The gesture was innocently erotic, sending a flash of arousal through Maddie. It took a couple of moments to return her attention to his words. "I've got to settle on my car first thing. I've got this big family gathering this afternoon. I have to pick up a few things at my hotel for the nieces and nephews, change my clothes, that kind of thing. Listen, don't fuss with coffee on my account. I can get a cup on my way over to the garage."

His hand remained on his bronzed, muscular chest, and Maddie had a hard time pulling her gaze away. It took great effort to meet his eyes, and she was both certain and embarrassed that Michael could guess at her unbusinesslike thoughts. "I was going to make it for myself, anyway."

"Well, then, coffee would be great."

"Okay."

There was a tension in his features. He was being pushed by opposing forces—his head telling him to get out while the going was good, his heart telling him to stick around the captivating Maddie Sargent just awhile longer. Slowly he let out a breath. "I won't be more than a few minutes."

Ten minutes later, showered and dressed, his dark hair combed and still damp, Michael reappeared in the kitchen. Maddie poured two cups of coffee.

"Milk? Sugar?"

Michael shook his head. "Black is fine. I used your hairbrush. And the toothpaste." He smiled crookedly. "Not the brush, though." He held up his index finger.

Maddie smiled back, handing him a cup. She sat across from him at the table, noticing that, all dressed in his formal business suit, he looked suddenly cool and distant. The clothes were not the whole reason, though. It was more the expression on his face, the aloof look in his deep blue eyes. He was once more the suave, self-assured, consummate businessman. She felt a sudden longing to recreate that feeling of cozy intimacy between them, but she sensed that he had removed himself from those feelings as surely as if he had already removed himself physically from her presence. His mind, no doubt, was already on his plans for the day, his family... perhaps even his intimate faux pas of the night before.

They drank their coffee in silence. Maddie had made some buttered toast, but it remained untouched on the table.

When Michael finished the cup, he hesitated before taking a second one. Maddie poured herself another half cup.

They started talking at the same time.

Michael laughed. "You first."

"I just wanted to be sure our date... I mean our business meeting," she quickly amended, "is set for tomorrow night. I know you'll probably be busy with your family this whole week, what with your sister's wedding and all."

She was giving him a perfect opening to wheedle out of the dinner, but Michael merely said somberly, "Tomorrow night is fine."

"Good." She took a sip of coffee and then reached for a slice of toast.

Michael followed suit. He studied her thoughtfully as he chewed.

"What is it?"

"I was just thinking... that cream you used on Timmy... it really did the trick."

Maddie grinned. "You should see what it does for a woman's complexion. I hadn't actually thought of that cream for the Barrett's line since we've just come out with it, but we could work it in. What do you think?"

But Michael wasn't listening. Other thoughts were floating around in his head. "Huh?"

She decided the hell with playing by Michael's rules. Why not push a little? At least give him something to mull over. "I was saying we could add it to the Barrett's line."

Michael gulped down the rest of his coffee. "We'll . . . talk about it." He rose. "Well, I'd better get going. It isn't snowing now, and the plows have been out awhile. I shouldn't have too much trouble getting a cab."

Maddie glanced at the kitchen clock. It was nearly ten. "I'd better get dressed and go see about my car, as well. Maybe I can get it started again and not have to get it towed." Then she stopped, remembering Timmy. She couldn't leave him. But the idea of bundling him up, walking five blocks in the cold with him in her arms and then contending with her car was more than she could cope with.

Michael was able to read her mind. "I have an idea. Why don't I hike over to your car and see if I can get it started for you. If I can, I'll bring it back here."

Maddie wasn't about to refuse the offer. Instead, she thought of a perfect plan. "I'll get dressed in the meantime and get Timmy bundled up. If you can get the car back here, we can zip you over to pick up your car at the lot."

"No. That seems like more bother—"

"Hey, I owe you the ride. We both remember why your car got towed in the first place."

Michael laughed. "Okay. It's a deal."

Maddie's face lit up. "Only the first of many, I hope."

Michael continued to smile, but uncomfortably. "What kind of car and where did you leave it?"

Maddie gave him the particulars and the car keys, insisting he borrow one of her scarves, a dark blue one, for his trek.

"I'll phone you if I have a problem," he called out before stepping into the elevator.

When the telephone rang twenty minutes later, Maddie was sure it was Michael calling to tell her either he couldn't start the car or, worse still, couldn't find it.

It wasn't Michael. It was her assistant, Liz.

"Well, how did it go?" Liz asked without preamble.

"Don't ask."

"Bad?"

Maddie had to think about that.

"That bad?" Liz sucked in a breath.

"Well..."

"Maddie, come on. What happened?"

Maddie laughed. "Everything." She paused. "And nothing." Again she paused. "Well...not nothing. I mean...nothing in the way of a firm deal. But..."

"But! But what?"

Maddie picked a speck of lint off her caramel wool slacks. "He's a most unusual man."

"Unusual? As in strange?"

"No. No, not strange."

"Maddie, you don't sound like yourself. You're not making any sense. Maddie, what's wrong?"

Phone in hand, Maddie ambled over to the hall mirror. She gave herself a quick check, wondering if she should put on a bit more makeup. For a moment she forgot that Liz had asked her a question.

"Maddie?"

"Huh. Oh, nothing's wrong, Liz." She adjusted the cowl neck of her creamy-white sweater. "Well, unless we count having a baby to contend with."

Maddie thought she could almost hear Liz's mouth drop open. "A baby?" she gasped. "You're...pregnant?" Liz gulped down some air. "But, Maddie...I didn't even know you were dating anyone."

"What? Oh, Liz. Of course I'm not dating anyone. And I'm not pregnant. I've just...got this baby... temporarily. And let me tell you, Liz, having a baby is no picnic. If it weren't for Michael..."

"Michael, huh? My, my, we've moved to first names quickly."

Maddie couldn't help laughing. Or saying, "We've moved quicker than that."

"Maddie! You've got to be kidding."

Maddie scowled. "What does that mean? Do you think I'm...I'm a saint or something?"

"Maddie, come on. You've got...well, you've always talked a good line about never mixing business with pleasure."

"I wouldn't say mix." Maddie smoothed an invisible line at the corner of her mouth. "Let's say...stirred lightly."

"What does that mean?"

"It means..." Maddie stopped. She leaned closer to the mirror, scrutinizing herself. "What does it mean?" There was a worried tone in her voice. "I don't know what it means, Liz. I think...it means...I'm in trouble." She looked her reflection square in the eye. "Liz, I'm sorry to say I lost my perspective last night. I broke...well, I almost broke a cardinal rule. You're right. I mean I'm right. It's absolutely foolhardy to mix business with pleasure. At least Michael...Mr. Harrington..." How could she call him Mr. Harrington after she'd spent practically half the morning snuggled in his arms? "Michael feels the same way. He's as dedicated to his work as I am to mine. And he's not about to complicate matters by getting personally involved with one of his clients."

"Then he offered you a deal?"

"Not exactly. Not yet. But he's definitely taken with our products. I used one on Timmy and—"

"Who's Timmy?"

"The baby I'm minding," Maddie said impatiently. "Anyway, Michael was amazed at how well it worked on the baby's bottom."

"Hold on, Maddie. Aren't you working the wrong age group, to say nothing of the wrong end? We're not supposed to be selling Harrington on how well the Sargent formula works on a baby's tush."

Maddie laughed. "Well, Michael was impressed nonetheless. I'm sure he's thinking that if it does wonders for a baby, it can do as well, if not better, for the Barrett's customer." Maddie heard a car horn beep outside. "Listen, that may be Michael honking for me. I'd better go. I'll see you tomorrow morning."

Maddie hung up before Liz could ask any more questions. The truth was, she had very few answers. No. The truth was, she didn't even want to ponder the questions right now.

She ran to the living-room window, delighted to see Michael step out of her car and wave to her. She opened the window.

"Hurry on down. I'm in another tow-away zone."

Maddie waved back. "Be right there."

It actually took a good five minutes to bundle up a groggy Timmy and pack an extra diaper, an emergency bottle, his rattle and a change of clothes . . . just in case. By the time she was done, he was most unhappy and let her know it in no uncertain terms. And by the time she rode the elevator down to the lobby, a screaming Timmy in her arms, Maddie had a first-rate headache. Then she had her first piece of good luck. Who should be coming in the front door but Mrs. Johnston, home from her visit to her daughter.

Maddie must have looked desperate. Without a word her neighbor took Timmy in her arms. "Shhhh. Shhhh. What's the matter, sweetheart? What's the matter?"

"I don't think he likes the idea of taking a little trip. I've got a . . . friend outside I have to give a lift to."

"So what if I take the baby with me? I'll watch him while you're gone."

"Oh, Mrs. Johnston, that would be great. I won't be long."

"Long. Short. It's all right. I'll be happy to have the company. I don't have to be anywhere until later in the afternoon."

"Oh, I won't be more than forty-five minutes," Maddie assured her.

"Anytime."

"He's only with me until tomorrow," Maddie said, holding up her hand to reveal her crossed fingers.

Already Timmy seemed less upset. And as Mrs. Johnston unwrapped him from the blanket and unzipped the front of his snowsuit, he was practically smiling.

"Thanks, Mrs. Johnston," Maddie said, handing over the tote with Timmy's things, then running across the lobby when she heard her horn beeping again.

She smiled at Michael as she stepped into the car. "You got it started. I'm amazed."

"Where's Timmy?" Michael asked worriedly.

"Oh, my neighbor offered to watch him."

"What neighbor?"

Maddie gave Michael a teasing grin. "What's the matter, Dad? Worried about the little tyke not being well looked after?"

Michael frowned. "Very funny." As he gunned the engine and pulled away from the curb, the car fish-tailed.

Maddie laughed softly. They rode in silence for a while, Maddie's thoughts drifting into fantasy. After a couple of minutes she commented, "It must be nice to have big family gatherings. Getting together for celebrations. Everyone excited, involved."

"Oh, they're involved, all right." Michael laughed dryly. "There's nothing the Harrington family loves more than a wedding. Let's see, today's the family gala. Tuesday night a bunch of the out-of-town relatives show up and we rent the back room at Steak and Stein for a pig out. Thursday night is the informal dinner with the groom's folks. And then there's the rehearsal dinner on Friday night." Michael grimaced. "And Jessie's only number four. That still leaves Kelly and Alan to go."

Maddie silently noted that he excluded himself from the single but eligible count. "How do you know they plan to get married?"

"Alan's already looking. He's made it clear he wants a wife by the time he finishes medical school. He'll find himself one, or my mother will. He's the only one of the kids that never minded Mom giving out his name and number to her friends' nieces or daughters." Michael laughed. "He's a mother's dream. And as for Kelly, the baby of the family, she's already making noises about getting hitched to this guy she's been seeing since her freshman year. The deal is, though, that she finishes college first."

"Who does she have that deal with?" Maddie asked.

"With me," Michael answered sharply. "Of all the kids, Kelly's got the most on the ball. She could really go places. I'm trying to get her to put marriage on extended hold and go to graduate school, get her MBA." He shook his head. "She's still such a baby sometimes. Spoiled rotten." He said the words with clear affection.

Maddie smiled wistfully, knowing it was Michael who'd spoiled her. She felt a flash of envy. How nice to be spoiled, protected and adored by a loving older brother. How nice to be a member of a large, close-knit family.

"What's the matter?" Michael asked, giving her a quick glance.

"I envy you, Michael," she said in a low voice.

Michael stole another look, nodded and maneuvered the car onto Storrow Drive. After a minute or two he said, "I have a confession to make."

"Oh?"

"I picked up a postcard that your mother sent to you. From Greece. The one with a Mr. Universe on the front. I guess curiosity got the best of me."

"She's funny," Maddie said thoughtfully, not the least bothered by Michael's admission. In a way, she liked the fact that he was curious about her. "Felicity is the most self-reliant, independent, contented career woman I've ever known. She loves gallivanting around the world, making her own decisions, being unencumbered. Oh, she's had men in her life, but they always came in a far second." She paused, wondering for a moment if that put her an even more distant third on her mother's list of priorities.

She shrugged. Those kinds of thoughts only depressed her. "I was raised to believe that being your own woman was the most important lesson to be learned. It was Felicity's idea that I start my own business. She backed me financially and emotionally. I don't mind telling you I was overwhelmed at first. She was terrific, though. One thing about Felicity. She knows how to run the show. And she taught me to be decisive, look confident even when I was shaking in my shoes, and believe in what I was doing. I don't think I could have pulled it off without her. It's the first time I remember her really coming through for me. But the crazy thing is, ever since the company really started taking off, just when you'd think she'd be cheering me on the most, she's been on my case to . . . well, you read the card."

"All mothers seem to have this natural instinct—"

"Not Felicity. She's not like other mothers, believe me. That's why I can't figure this new campaign she's on to get me fixed up. Sometimes I wonder if she's jealous of me. Maybe she figures a *good man* could drag me down a few notches."

Michael gave her a curious look. "Is that what having a man in your life would do?"

Maddie studied him as he returned his gaze to the road. "Don't you think so? I mean, aren't you just as worried that a personal involvement would drag you down?"

"Well, there's always that risk. But that's not what worries me. What worries me is having more demands made on me, having someone want things from me that I don't have the time or the inclination to give. I've got enough tugs on me, contending with my family. Barrett's been on me for the past year to move to the new offices here in Boston. No way. Having a nonstop diet of Harrington woes, dilemmas and hassles is just what I went to New York to escape."

"Maybe it's time to tell them you want out of the daddy role." She paused. "Or *do* you want out?"

Michael opened his mouth to protest but closed it without saying anything. A minute later they were exiting Storrow Drive. The car lot was just a block from the exit.

Maddie slid over to the driver's seat as Michael stepped out and closed the door. Rolling down the window, Maddie asked, "Shall I wait and make sure everything's okay?"

Michael pressed both hands on the window ledge and leaned down so he could see her face. "No, that's okay. Listen, Maddie, thanks." He tapped his fingers nervously against the metal.

"I should thank you. I mean, for helping me with Timmy. For not thinking I'm . . . ditsy. For giving me a second chance."

He stared at her in silence. "Well, I'll see you tomorrow night, then."

"I'll be there. Have a nice time today, Michael."

His brow furrowed. "Yeah. Thanks." He started to straighten up, then bent down again. "You, too." He smiled. "You should be okay. You've got down the bottle and the diapering bit. Yeah . . . you'll do great."

"Don't forget to pick up those gifts for your nieces and nephews."

He rapped lightly on the car door. "Right. I won't forget. Those kids would attack if their old uncle showed up empty-handed. They'll attack, anyway. Wrestling me to the floor is one of their favorite pastimes."

Maddie laughed softly. "Sounds like fun." She released the emergency brake. "Well, I'd better get back and see to Timmy."

Michael rapped lightly on the car again, gave her one more lingering look and then strode off at a vigorous pace.

AN HOUR LATER Michael was driving toward his hotel. He kept thinking about Maddie, his fingers toying with her scarf. He knew they had dinner plans for the next night. He knew it was crazy to be thinking that tomorrow night seemed a long time away. Of course, he could stop by her place and give her back her scarf. But that was a pretty lame excuse, considering he could give it to her the next evening. He was just coming up to her exit on Storrow Drive. Okay, so it was a lame excuse. He couldn't come up with a better one.

Maddie was just finishing a very proficient diapering job on Timmy when she heard a horn beeping outside. She ignored the first few blasts and then peered out the window.

Michael stepped out of his red sports car and waved to her, the borrowed scarf in his hand.

She opened the window.

"I forgot to return this."

"You could have waited till tomorrow night. I have another one," Maddie called down.

He crossed his arms over his chest for warmth and stared up at her with a grim, perplexed look on his face, thinking that he must be crazy. He called out, "Hey, look, I've talked your ear off about the Harrington brood. You might as well come along and meet them."

Maddie felt like a schoolgirl who'd been asked to the prom just when she'd given up hope of ever getting there. "You want me to come to your family gathering?"

He looked up at Maddie, who was flushed, beautiful, excited. "Yeah, why not?"

"Well . . . okay . . . great." And then she remembered. "What about Timmy? I can't impose on Mrs. Johnston again."

"So bring him."

Maddie eyed him speculatively. But then, afraid he'd change his mind and not at all sure why she was making such a big deal of the invitation, she quickly shouted, "Okay, I'll be right down."

6

AT TWO-FIFTEEN Michael was edging into a tight spot in front of a newly painted, gray clapboard, two-story house on a street lined with houses of similar ilk and upkeep. Only the color of clapboard varied. A long driveway ran up the right side of each house. Most had one or two cars parked in them, safely off the recently plowed street. But Mrs. Harrington's driveway contained six cars, packed bumper-to-bumper or squeezed in sideways. The rear end of the last one, a large blue sedan, edged out into the street.

Michael managed after a couple of tries to fit into the small space. Maddie glanced over at him as he shut off the ignition. There were beads of sweat across his brow that she didn't think came from the exertion of maneuvering the powerful Lamborghini into the parking space.

She took a shaky breath, watching as Michael remained behind the wheel fidgeting with his keys.

Timmy enjoyed the demonstration, his baby-blue eyes watching the jingling keys with fascination. Maddie wasn't entranced.

"Look, Michael, if you're having second thoughts..." She paused for a moment hoping for a speedy contradiction, but none came. "I could tuck Timmy under my coat and trudge through a few ten-foot snowdrifts down to Dorchester Boulevard and try to hail a cab."

He slowly turned his head and stared at her, a faint smile on his lips that Maddie couldn't read.

"It's just . . . they're . . . likely to make a big fuss." He smiled a touch more broadly, but it was forced.

"A fuss about what?"

He merely sighed. "It's just the way they are. I don't . . . make it a habit of bringing women to family get-togethers. My family can get . . . carried away."

"Well, maybe when you bring a date. But this is different. I mean . . . I'm a . . . a business client. They can't make very much of that, can they?"

Michael stared at Timmy. "No, right."

Maddie tilted her head. "You think they'll mind about the baby?"

Michael raised his eyes to her face. "Mind? Last count there were five nieces and nephews, and you never know when another one is about to arrive. Timmy will fit right into the baby set." He could feel himself relaxing a little. It was ridiculous to feel so uptight about bringing Maddie. She was right. How big a deal would they make over his inviting a business client along? Besides, he knew that Maddie would get a big kick out of an afternoon with the boisterous, affectionate Harrington clan. And when he thought about having to tell her tomorrow evening that he'd chosen to give L'Amour the contract, he hoped Maddie would be less likely to feel there was anything personal in his decision.

He smiled at her. "All set?"

She laughed nervously. "You're sure they won't feel I'm intruding?" She stared down at her camel wool slacks. "Maybe I should have changed. Put on a skirt . . ."

He leaned over, touched her cheek lightly and then squeezed Timmy's pudgy thigh, which was thickly wrapped in a blanket and his snowsuit. "You both look terrific, Maddie. It will be fine, you'll see."

Maddie swallowed, managing a not-too-convincing smile.

Michael got out of the car, sloshed through the wet snow near the curb around to Maddie's side, opened her door, reached in for Timmy, then helped her out with his free hand.

He watched Maddie's slender legs clad in trim slacks climb the steps to the front door as he followed with Timmy in his arms. She had beautiful legs, he thought. The kind of legs that look good in slacks. But he'd enjoyed his view of them more last night when she'd worn a dress. Great legs. He found himself wishing he'd stayed with her at her place today, given in to his erotic impulses, let his fingers glide languorously up and down those luscious legs....

Maddie stopped abruptly on the second last step. Michael, lost in illicit thoughts, nearly bumped into her.

"What's wrong?"

His voice sounded shaky. Maddie mistakenly read it as nerves.

"The packages. You left the packages for your family in the trunk." She could see little white puffs of breath drifting out of her mouth and Michael's as they spoke.

"Oh, right." He started to turn.

"Wait, let me take Timmy."

Michael nodded absently, passing the baby to her. He was still working at tempering those unbidden fantasies that kept springing up on him at the most unexpected times.

He hurried back to the car, and Maddie waited on the step. She watched Michael retrieve the packages. Then she glanced up at the front door to Mrs. Harrington's house. Her knees felt a little weak. She eyed Timmy, who seemed to be enjoying the crisp, cold air. And then she frowned.

Michael was coming back up the steps. "What is it?"

"I didn't bring any diapers for Timmy. I completely forgot."

"Don't worry. Lee or Debby will have some. They both still have kids in diapers."

"I feel so stupid."

She looked downcast. And Michael knew she was nervous. He smiled at her. "It's okay. You're new at the game."

Maddie shifted Timmy in her arms and smiled back.

For an instant Michael felt a funny sensation. *This is what it would be like to have a wife and kid and be arriving at Mom's for a family bash.* His own family. He caught Maddie's eye. Her smile deepened. He felt an urge to take her hand. But she was clutching Timmy, and he had an armload of packages. And then he heard the faint sounds of voices from inside the house. The warm feeling ended with a jolt. There was a thickening in his throat, a knot in his stomach. No, it was all wrong. A wife? A kid? Him? Michael Harrington? No. No way. What's wrong with this picture, folks? His eyes swept over Maddie and Timmy. Everything.

He scrambled up the rest of the steps and walked across the porch to the front door, leaving Maddie to follow his lead. His large frame just about blocked her and Timmy from view as he swung open the door. "Hey, the prodigal son has returned. Where is everybody?"

From down the hall came happy shouts from little children.

"It's Uncle Mike."

"Nana, Uncle Mike's finally here."

Two little boys and a little girl came bounding down the hall, trying to race each other to the prize—their uncle.

A young woman stepped out of the same room the children had come from and into the hall. "Hey, slow down, kids, don't bowl him over. Give the poor guy a chance...."

Michael bent, and Maddie and Timmy came into view for the first time. It was like someone had pulled out the plug of a movie projector in the middle of an action scene. Everyone froze, the children nearly tumbling over each other as they came to a grinding stop. The woman at the end of the hall didn't finish her sentence, didn't move.

The silence only lasted for a few moments, but to Maddie and Michael it felt endless.

"Cindy?" came a woman's voice from inside the room. "What's the matter?" As she finished her sentence, she, too, appeared in the hallway. She was an older woman with graying hair, tall and stocky, and she wore a blue-checked apron over her navy dress.

"Michael?" She smiled broadly. "You brought company?" She turned her head so she could speak to the people remaining in the room she'd just exited. "He brought company."

Maddie had to edge forward a few more steps just so she could close the door behind her. In tense silence she watched the mass arrival into the hall.

"You son of a gun, Mike." A younger, bulkier version of Michael was the first to stride down the hall. "I don't believe it."

"Believe what, Alan?" Michael retorted gruffly.

The rest of the family—Maddie saw them as a troop of hundreds, but there were less than twenty of them—seemed to come to life at the sound of Michael's voice. They hurried down the hall en masse, and Maddie had a terrifying vision of being trampled by a horde of excited Harringtons.

Mrs. Harrington got to Maddie first. "Michael...yours?" Her voice quavered with anticipation as her large hand hovered over Timmy.

"Mine?" Michael's voice cracked. "Of course he's not mine." He stared at the wide-eyed sea of faces. "Whoa there, folks. Settle down. You're way off track here."

Maddie wasn't sure if Mrs. Harrington simply didn't hear Michael or if she chose not to believe him. Tears brimmed in her eyes. "A beautiful baby." And then she gazed at Maddie. "Beautiful."

"Mom!" Michael said, the word filled with exasperation. Then he roughly grabbed Maddie's jacket sleeve, edging her forward. "This is Maddie Sargent. A business client. We...were discussing...business this morning and...well, I just thought she might enjoy—" he stopped, scowled and then went on "—coming over."

"What a lovely baby," an attractive dark-haired woman with the Harrington blue eyes exclaimed. "Hi," she said, extending a hand to Maddie, "I'm Lee."

Maddie smiled nervously. "Hi."

"What's his name?" This came from a woman who introduced herself as Debby.

"Timmy."

"Here, let me take him," Mrs. Harrington said. "Set the packages down. You get your coats off. It's hot in here. You don't want to start sweating and come down with a cold."

They were both sweating plenty. Maddie gave Michael a wan smile, but he was busy eyeing his brother, Alan.

"Get that look off your face. I told you, Miss Sargent is a business client. Let's try to show her that the Harringtons are not a bunch of babbling idiots."

"Michael, such talk! Whoever she is, she's welcome. And so is her beautiful little boy."

Maddie cleared her throat. "Oh, he's not mine."

"No." Michael nodded. "I mean . . . she's right. He's not hers."

There were several awkward chuckles from the clan. "Hey, you two, relax." This from another blue-eyed Harrington woman. Then she addressed the brood. "You know Michael hates getting grilled, folks. Now let's just leave them be to get their bearings. Don't we have to get the table set, Mom?"

Mrs. Harrington was still beaming down at the baby in her arms. Then she smiled ruefully at her son. "Not yours. Not hers. What did you do? Pluck this sweet baby from a tree?"

Michael started to open his mouth to explain but merely sighed. "Please, Mom, just take Timmy inside and get his snowsuit off. He probably could use a diaper change...if there are any extras around." He looked awkwardly over at Maddie. "She . . . forgot to bring them."

Maddie grimaced. "I'm sorry."

"In a grandmother's house there are always plenty of diapers." She reached out and squeezed Maddie's arm.

"It's like that with the first. You forget. One time when Michael was a baby, I went to visit a friend and I actually went back home without him. I forgot I had a baby altogether. Was I embarrassed when my friend Francine called. You remember that story, Michael?"

"You've told it enough times, Mom," he said dryly.

Maddie was unzipping her jacket. "Really, Mrs. Harrington . . ." She started to explain about Timmy.

But the woman was already cooing to Timmy and heading down the hall, the rest of the Harrington clan following suit.

When they were all out of sight, Maddie gripped Michael's wrist. "They don't believe us," she said in amazement. "They think—"

"I know what they think," Michael snapped. "They think I knocked you up. They think Timmy is mine." He shook his head slowly. "They probably think they've got another wedding to plan." His eyes narrowed ominously. "This was a bad idea."

"I could make a run for it," Maddie muttered.

"What about our *son*? Grandma down there is already performing the Harrington initiation rites on him."

"Michael, you have to explain."

"Just let it ride. I know them too well. Explain and they'll just think I'm getting cold feet. Then they'll be rushing to your side, telling you how to snare me. Oh, they're pros. And they've been waiting with bated breath for something like this."

"Didn't you realize they'd get the wrong impression when you asked me to come?"

Michael stared morosely at her. "I wasn't thinking about them when I invited you."

Maddie smiled a little. "Oh." She took off her coat and bent to unzip her boots. She had to grip Michael's arm so she wouldn't lose her balance. When she touched him, she could feel him stiffen. "Come on, Michael. I'm sure we can convince them they're barking up the wrong tree."

Michael slipped off his coat and hung it on a hook. "We're not going to be too convincing if we stay huddled together here." He cocked his head. "Ready, Ms Sargent?"

Maddie lifted her chin, threw her shoulders back and smiled. "Ready, Mr. Harrington, sir."

GOSSIP, LAUGHTER and devouring heaping plates of baked ham, mashed potatoes and other assorted nourishments were the order of the day. After the first tentative half hour or so Maddie found herself having a gay old time. Michael's family was warm, effusive, funny and welcomed her into the fold as if she was a new member.

Which was exactly why Michael Harrington sat in silence most of the afternoon, wondering what had ever possessed him to bring Maddie here today. Every time one of the family cooed at Timmy or smiled adoringly at Maddie, his brows shot up, a disgruntled expression darkening his features. The worst part, though, was enduring the ribbing, the little digs, the less-than-subtle innuendos about Maddie and Timmy that all of his siblings delighted in imparting. What had Michael told Maddie last night? That one of these days he'd get his comeuppance? He was getting it in spades.

Maddie was enjoying herself too much to pay Michael much mind. She was charmed by the Harrington brood, charmed by this wonderful feeling of warmth and acceptance she had never really known. She loved the attention, the feeling of belonging . . . even if it was only temporary.

When she took Timmy into one of the bedrooms to change his diaper after dinner, Cindy, the eldest sister, joined her.

"He's being impossible, isn't he?" Cindy commented idly while Maddie undressed Timmy and fumbled with the tabs of the disposable diaper Michael's sister handed her.

Maddie smiled uncomfortably. "I guess I shouldn't have come."

"Nonsense. Anyway, it's about time Michael faced the music. We all knew he'd get to this point one of these days."

"Cindy, really, you've got it wrong. We're not an item. And I swear, Timmy really is my cousin's baby. The last thing in the world I need is a baby." Timmy giggled and Cindy smiled indulgently at Maddie, neither of them apparently convinced.

"I catch the way he keeps looking at you," Cindy said.

"Timmy?"

Cindy laughed. "Michael. I'd say that brother of mine is smitten."

"Smitten? That's crazy. If looks could kill . . ."

Cindy laughed. "When Mike can't play it cool with a woman, believe me, she's gotten to him." Cindy's blue eyes shone. "You've got to him, I should say." Only her limited acquaintance with Maddie prevented Cindy from adding that Maddie looked equally beguiled. She settled for saying, "He's a great catch, that brother of mine."

"Cindy, I only met Michael last night. And then, through an unbelievable comedy of errors, we...well, we got to know each other...a little better than we might have. But I really am his client. His potential client, that is. Michael's a frustratingly cagey businessman. But I guess that's why he's so successful."

"Oh, he's frustrated, all right." Cindy grinned.

"You haven't bought a thing I've said." Maddie had gone from struggling with the diaper tabs to struggling with fitting the diaper on Timmy.

"Here, let me. With two kids, I'm a pro." Cindy nudged Maddie and took over, quickly diapering the baby and redressing him with equal speed. "There, nothing to it." Cindy picked up Timmy and smiled at Maddie. "It doesn't matter when the two of you met. Or whether you're a client of Mike's or not. I'm closer to Mike than anyone else in the family. I know the person behind that successful, cagey businessman facade. I know he's taken with you, just as I know about his tenderness, his commitment to all of us, his sacrifices and what they cost him. I even know about the resentment he tries to hide, the anger he feels at all his missed opportunities. Mike's biggest problem is that he holds everything in. He needs to let go, have some fun, stop taking life so seriously."

Maddie sat down on the edge of the bed. "He mentioned having had some dreams when he was growing up."

Cindy gave Maddie a sly look. "My, my. That reticent brother of mine is certainly loquacious around a woman he only just met."

"Aha," Maddie said smugly, "but he refused to tell me what those dreams were about."

Cindy laughed. "Give him time. I'm sure he'll get around to telling you. Mike was a star athlete in high school. Especially basketball."

"He used to go to all the Celtics games with your dad."

Cindy eyed Maddie shrewdly. "He told you that, too."

"Big deal. We both talked a little about our families, about growing up."

"Oh, but it *is* a big deal. Michael never talks about himself very much. And just about never about dad. We all took my father's death very hard, but no one as hard as Michael. He seemed to change overnight. He became so driven, so intense. He got it into his head that, single-handedly, he was going to make it up to all of us. For a long time he blamed himself. None of us could convince him that he wasn't somehow responsible for Dad's heart attack."

Maddie's brows knit. "Why would Michael feel responsible? He was at school when it happened." Maddie saw the look of surprise on Cindy's face. "I guess," Maddie admitted, "we both talked more openly to each other than we usually do. But why, Cindy? Why would Michael blame himself?"

Cindy regarded Maddie. "Mike and Dad were fooling around the day before, playing street hockey. When they came in for supper, Dad was real sweaty, and Mom bawled him out for carrying on like he was still a kid." Cindy looked down. "They fooled around like that all the time. Basketball was the main activity, though. Dad's biggest dream—and Mike's—was that Mike would play pro basketball one day. Mike was that good."

Timmy started to fuss a little, and Maddie took him from Cindy, absently rubbing his back, soothing him.

"Did Mike tell you that he won a full basketball scholarship to Northwestern?" Cindy asked.

Maddie shook her head.

"Then, until this moment, I'm probably the only person Mike told. He burned the letter the day it arrived, before Mom got home from work."

"But why?"

"Mom would have insisted he go, of course. And he didn't tell the rest of the kids because he never wanted them to feel that he was making any big sacrifices or anything by turning it down. That's the way Mike is."

"Michael told me that there wasn't money for college. But if he got a full scholarship . . ."

"Mom was barely making ends meet on her salary. Mike never considered going to college. He felt he had to get a full-time job and help support the family. He's still carrying more than his share. Who do you think paid off the mortgage on this house for Mom? Who do you think is paying for Alan's education? Kelly's? Who do you think is footing most of the bill for Jessie's wedding?"

So much for Michael Harrington's claim to not being selfless, Maddie thought. She said softly, "He's a special person."

Cindy observed her in silence for a few moments. "I know how terrified Mike is of taking on any more responsibilities. From the time he was seventeen or so, he swore he'd never get married, never get too involved with any woman. He's kept to that promise. Up to now. But there's not a single person in this house—except maybe you and Michael—who doesn't know something hot is brewing. You couldn't find a better man

than Michael Harrington, Maddie. He was meant to be
a husband and father."

"Look, don't get me wrong. I think Michael is a terrific man. But all I want from him is a contract to fea-
ture a line of my skin-care products at Barrett's. I'm not
looking for a husband. And, believe me, I'm not looking for a father for my children. I mean . . . I don't want
any children. I don't want a husband. I don't want to
get . . . involved." She shook her head vigorously. "Michael and me? Never. We're both workaholics. I own a
business that takes complete commitment, total dedi-
cation. There's no room in my life for anything else.
Certainly not a husband or a baby."

Cindy merely smiled, and Maddie returned the gesture with a look of frustration. Maddie stood up,
hoisting Timmy in her arms. "We'd better get back.
Your mom said something about dessert."

Cindy nodded, taking silent note of the tender little
smile that lit Maddie's face as Timmy giggled. She also
noted the way Maddie tempered that smile when she
realized she'd been caught in the act of being maternal.

There was coffee, several pies, cookies and a large
chocolate cake on the dining-room table. When Maddie entered with Timmy, Kelly grabbed the baby and
shooed all the children into the front parlor, where she
was taking charge of handing out milk and cookies and
giving the rest of the adults some peace and quiet.

Michael, leaning against the wall in a corner, had
never been as quiet or felt as awkward at a family gathering. He turned down a slice of cake and mumbled
something about having to get Maddie home. When he
tried to turn down a slice of cake for Maddie, his mother
wouldn't hear of it. And Maddie was no help. "Why,

this looks delicious, Mrs. Harrington," she said brightly.

"Please, call me Anne."

Maddie smiled, catching the flicker of frustration in Michael's face. She knew Michael was eager to leave, but she refused to let him spoil the day for her. She wasn't likely to have another like this. From the uneasy look on Michael's face, she doubted she'd get a second invitation to a family gathering.

As it turned out she was wrong. But the second invitation didn't come from Michael. Before they left, Jessica insisted Maddie come to her wedding on Saturday. The rest of the family enthusiastically seconded the invitation.

IN THE CAR DRIVING BACK, Maddie glanced over at Michael. "It would have been rude to turn them down."

"Did I say anything?" he muttered.

Maddie shrugged. "I thought it was very nice of Jessica to invite me to her wedding."

Michael didn't respond, his eyes fixed straight ahead, his expression distant.

They drove the rest of the way in silence. That is, Maddie and Michael were silent. Timmy, on the other hand, counterpointed the silence with intermittent shrieks, cries and general irritation. Maybe the tension was getting to him, Maddie thought, almost envying the baby for being able to deal with his feelings so expressively. Then again, maybe it wasn't the tension in the car. Maybe it was his diaper rash. So much for her wonder cream.

Michael pulled up in front of her apartment building and glanced at her. "Can you manage?"

Maddie observed him. For all Cindy had said about her brother being tender, caring, sensitive, and for all that Maddie believed her, right now she thought Michael Harrington insufferable. "I can manage just fine, thank you."

He started to reach across her to open the door, but Maddie's hand got to the handle first. She swung her legs out.

"Wait." Michael's tone was low.

She turned expectantly, hoping for an apology. Or at least a kind word.

"Your scarf." He still had it stuffed in his coat pocket.

"That's all right," Maddie said, her hands full with Timmy. "Bring it tomorrow night."

"About tomorrow night . . ."

Maddie's eyes widened. She couldn't believe he'd renege on the meeting simply because of his family's positive reaction to her.

"The thing is—" Michael rubbed his neck "—there are still a few issues regarding the contract that haven't been resolved back at the home office. This . . . meeting . . . may be premature. Why don't I . . . call you? I might even fly back to New York for a couple of days. Look into a few things."

"I see," Maddie said tightly.

Michael watched her struggle for a moment to hold on to a squirming Timmy and get out of the low-slung sports car.

"Here . . . wait. Let me help you," Michael said, throwing open his car door.

"I don't need any help," Maddie muttered, managing with a lack of grace to extricate herself.

... be tempted!

See inside for special
4 FREE BOOKS offer

Discover deliciously different
romance with 4 Free Novels from

Harlequin Temptation ®

Sit back and enjoy four exciting romances—yours **FREE** from Harlequin Reader Service! But wait . . . there's *even more* to this great offer!

A Useful, Practical Digital Clock/Calendar—FREE

As a free gift simply to thank you for accepting four free books we'll send you a stylish digital quartz clock/calendar—a handsome addition to any decor! The changeable, month-at-a-glance calendar pops out, and may be replaced with a favorite photograph.

PLUS A FREE MYSTERY GIFT—a surprise bonus that will delight you!

All this just for trying our Reader Service!

MONEY-SAVING HOME DELIVERY

Once you receive 4 FREE books and gifts, you'll be able to preview more great romance reading in the convenience of your own home at less than retail prices. Every month we'll deliver 4 brand-new Harlequin Temptation novels right to your door months before they appear in stores. If you decide to keep them, they'll be yours for only $2.24 each! That's 26¢ less per book than the retail price—with no additional charges for home delivery. And you may cancel at any time, for any reason, and still keep your free books and gifts, just by dropping us a line!

SPECIAL EXTRAS—FREE

You'll also get our newsletter with each shipment, packed with news of your favorite authors and upcoming books—FREE! And as a valued reader, we'll be sending you additional free gifts from time to time—as a token of our appreciation.

BE TEMPTED! COMPLETE, DETACH AND MAIL YOUR POSTPAID ORDER CARD TODAY AND RECEIVE 4 FREE BOOKS, A DIGITAL CLOCK/CALENDAR AND MYSTERY GIFT—PLUS LOTS MORE!

A FREE
Digital Clock/Calendar
and Mystery Gift *await you, too!*

Harlequin Temptation®

Harlequin Reader Service ®
901 Fuhrmann Blvd., P.O. Box 1867, Buffalo, NY14240-9952

☐ **YES!** Please rush me my four Harlequin Temptation novels with my FREE Digital Clock/Calendar and Mystery Gift. As explained on the opposite page, I understand that I am under no obligation to purchase any books. The free books and gifts remain mine to keep.

142 CIH MDRR

_____
NAME   (please print)

_____
ADDRESS   APT.

_____
CITY   STATE   ZIP CODE

Offer limited to one per household and not valid to current Temptation subscribers. Prices subject to change.

HARLEQUIN READER SERVICE "NO-RISK" GUARANTEE

- There's no obligation to buy—and the free books and gifts remain yours to keep.
- You pay the lowest price possible and receive books before they appear in stores.
- You may end your subscription anytime—just write and let us know.

If offer card is missing, write to: Harlequin Reader Service, 901 Fuhrman Blvd., P.O. Box 1867, Buffalo, NY 14269-1867

Clip and mail this postpaid card today!

BUSINESS REPLY CARD

First Class   Permit No. 717   Buffalo, NY

Postage will be paid by addressee

Harlequin Reader Service
901 Fuhrmann Blvd.
P.O. BOX 1867
BUFFALO, NY 14240-9952

NO POSTAGE
NECESSARY
IF MAILED
IN THE
UNITED STATES

Michael got out, anyway, catching up to her and grabbing her arm as she trudged with Timmy, her purse and the tote bag over a pile of snow along the curb.

"Maddie..."

They were at the front of the building. "Yes."

He stared at Timmy, and then at her, an unreadable expression on his face. "I will get back to you." Without another word he turned and headed for his car.

7

"PLEASE, MADDIE. I know it's asking a lot, but Donald and I need a little more time. I promise I'll be back no later than Friday."

"But, Linda, I've got to go to work. I have a business to run. I expected you back this morning. What do I do about Timmy?" Maddie picked up her dress from the bed and tried to slip it on over her head and hang on to the receiver at the same time.

"Couldn't you get someone in to watch him during the day? I'll pay for it."

"It's not the money," Maddie muttered, staring down at Timmy, who was rolling over onto his belly on the carpet, precariously close to the bookcase. "Oh, hold on a minute," Maddie said, dropping the receiver, grabbing Timmy and setting him on her queen-size bed. She gave him her key ring for amusement. Timmy giggled with delight, and Maddie grinned down at him, almost forgetting the discarded receiver for a moment.

"Sorry, Linda." She sat down at the edge of the bed. Timmy's little hands alternated between jingling the key ring and stroking the back of Maddie's silk dress. She winked at him over her shoulder. "Oh, well, I guess I could call a baby-sitting agency," she said slowly. "Timmy does seem to be settling down. But you might have told me he has colic."

"Colic? Timmy doesn't have colic. He's almost never cranky. Well, I guess he was pretty fussy when I handed him over to you, but I'm sure he was just picking up on my upset."

"He cried half of last night. It sounded like colic to me. Oh, and he had a bad case of diaper rash. I used one of my new skin-care products on him, though, and the rash cleared up completely."

"Timmy does get diaper rash sometimes. But to tell you the truth, I've tried half a dozen baby ointments on him, and none of them seems to work very well. You'll have to give me a tube of your stuff when I get back."

"Sure. Anyway, he's fine now," Maddie said, a touch of pride in her voice. She reached around and tickled Timmy's tummy, much to the baby's delight. "I'd better go. I'll have to phone my assistant and have her hold the fort till I track down a sitter for Timmy. Actually, I have a neighbor who might do it. If not," she said more to herself than to Linda, her eyes fixed on the smiling baby, "I guess I could stick around the house and catch up on some paperwork."

"Thanks, Maddie. You're an angel."

Timmy caught hold of Maddie's finger, gripping it in his little fist. "Well," Maddie told Timmy as she hung up, "I guess it won't be so bad playing mamma for a few more days."

Twenty minutes later Maddie wished she could eat her words. Timmy was crying hysterically and Maddie realized the brooch that had been pinned on her dress before she put it on was missing.

She hadn't put the two together until she checked Timmy's diaper to make sure the rash hadn't returned and the safety pins on his diaper were secure. Then she thoroughly searched her floor and her bed for the missing brooch.

"No, no," she muttered, her search growing more frantic as Timmy's shrieks grew louder. "Oh, God, no." There was a pleading note in her voice as she picked up Timmy, trying to comfort him. She grabbed his half-finished bottle from the bureau. "Come on, Timmy. You're just thirsty, right?"

Wrong. Timmy winced in pain as Maddie stuck the nipple in his mouth.

In her panic her first thought was to call Michael. Michael was an expert with kids. Michael would know what to do. *If only he's still at his hotel . . .* she thought, frantically looking up the number and then dialing, a flood of relief filling her when he answered the phone on the fourth ring. He'd barely gotten out a hello when she exploded into a rush of words.

"Maddie, calm down. I can't make out a word of what you're saying." Michael set his suitcase down. He'd been halfway out the door when he heard the phone ring. "What's Timmy screaming about?"

"That's what I'm trying to tell you," she shouted into the receiver, on the verge of hysterics herself as she paced with the sobbing baby. "He swallowed my brooch, Michael"

Michael frowned. "Your brooch?"

"It was on my dress. But it's not there now. I had the dress on the bed this morning before I started getting dressed. And then Linda called. And I was trying to get my dress on. She isn't coming back. I mean . . . not for a while. Oh, what am I going to do about Timmy, Michael? I'd better call the police. An ambulance."

"Maddie, calm down. Did you see Timmy swallow your brooch?" He spoke in a low, soothing voice, his chief concern at the moment to keep Maddie from panicking.

"No, no. But he did, Michael. I'm sure of it. I'd better take him to the hospital. Should I do something for him first?"

"The first thing to do is take a few deep breaths. If he's shrieking like that, we know he isn't choking. Just hold still. I'll drive over and get you. I was just on my way out the door, anyway, and my car's waiting out front. We'll take him down to Children's Hospital and let them check Timmy out. But look, Timmy could have indigestion or a cold or be cutting a tooth. It's not too likely he swallowed a piece of jewelry."

"Oh, Michael . . ."

"Keep looking for that brooch of yours, though. I'll be there as fast as I can."

Maddie was down in the lobby with a still-shrieking Timmy in her arms when Michael pulled up less than ten minutes later. She rushed out to the car, brushing away her own tears as she got in with the baby.

Michael put a comforting arm around her, gave Timmy a quick pat on the back and pulled out fast. Fifteen minutes later he was sitting with his arm around Maddie again, this time in the emergency waiting room, while a doctor examined Timmy.

"It's all my fault." Maddie used Michael's hanky to wipe her eyes.

"First of all, we don't know that Timmy swallowed the brooch. Second, it isn't as if you set Timmy down with the dress and let him merrily play with the brooch. You said you already had your dress on when you put Timmy on the bed."

"But I should have spotted that the brooch was missing. I should have been more careful. I should have watched him more closely. I should have—"

Michael cut her off sharply. "Maddie, there's no point in 'should haves.' Believe me, I know."

Maddie watched him take her hand. She met his dark blue eyes, so tender now, and she remembered her conversation yesterday with Michael's sister Cindy. Michael had blamed himself for his father's heart attack. No doubt he had been tormented by many "should haves," too. She squeezed his hand, her pale lips curving in a weak semblance of a smile.

"Thank you, Michael. You keep coming through for me. You probably think I'm a complete incompetent at this point."

He stroked her tear-stained cheek and then hugged her closer to him. "I don't think anything of the sort. I think you're terrific, Maddie Sargent."

A passing nurse caught Michael's remark and smiled, a clear touch of envy in her expression. Maddie smiled, too, her smile tinged with a mix of pleasure and trepidation. Michael pressed Maddie's head to his shoulder, his lips finding their way to her honey-hued hair.

They were still sitting like that when the doctor entered with Timmy, now subdued, in his arms.

Both Maddie and Michael sprang up from the plastic seats in unison, concerned expressions etched on their faces.

The doctor smiled. "We X-rayed him. No sign of a silver brooch. I have a feeling that it'll turn up one of these days."

"But . . . he was crying so hard. And he looked like he was in real pain," Maddie said.

The doctor handed Timmy over to her. "Oh, he *is* in pain. But not from swallowing a brooch."

Maddie stared at him, a look of terror on her face, waiting to hear the doctor's diagnosis.

Michael gripped Maddie's hand. "What's wrong with Timmy?"

The doctor's smile broadened. "Relax, it's just an ear infection. It's very likely been coming on for a few days now. Has he been fussier than usual, tugging at his ears? That's often the case."

Maddie nodded and smiled sheepishly. "I thought it might be an allergy . . . to me."

The doctor grinned. "You two must be new parents, right?"

Michael and Maddie shared a private look but said nothing.

"I'll write out a prescription for an antibiotic in liquid form. You'll have to give it to Timmy three times a day. He should be feeling much better in twenty-four hours. I already administered the first dose here, and he's starting to settle down. The only problem you may have is that some babies do get diarrhea from the medication and then develop a bad case of diaper rash."

Michael grinned at Maddie. "Don't worry, doc. We've got that end covered."

On the way home Michael stopped to fill the prescription while Maddie called Liz at the office to tell her she'd be working at home for the day. And yes, in answer to Liz's question, she was still playing mama.

When they arrived at Maddie's place, she started to thank Michael and say goodbye. He'd told her during the drive back that he'd planned to catch a plane to New York that morning, and she assumed he'd want to get out to the airport as soon as possible. While she was disappointed that it meant definitely canceling their business dinner for that night, she was feeling too grateful to Michael for helping her with Timmy to balk.

He'd promised to return in a few days, and she was still hopeful they'd firm up a deal.

Michael, however, insisted on coming up with her, and Maddie didn't argue. Timmy was fussing again, pulling on his ears, and she felt that familiar helpless feeling. Michael took him from her, and when they entered her apartment, Michael slipped off his coat, undid Timmy's snowsuit and paced the hall with him in an attempt to settle the child down. Maddie was about to put on some coffee for them when the doorbell rang.

She opened the door to find Mrs. Johnston standing there. "I stopped by to see if you wanted me to watch Timmy until his mother comes back today. I thought you'd probably need to get to work. He's no trouble." Mrs. Johnston peered down the hall at Michael and the sobbing baby. "Oh, dear, still fussy."

"He's got an ear infection. I just got back from the doctor. He said Timmy needs to take an antibiotic, so I'm going to stay home with him." She chose not to mention her initial panic about Timmy swallowing the missing brooch.

"Oh, don't worry. It's not serious. My daughter's baby just got over an ear infection." Mrs. Johnston smiled at Maddie, who was still pale and frazzled. "You look like you could use a break. I'm home all day with nothing to do. Why don't you let me take Timmy for a few hours and give you a chance to relax?"

"I have to give him his medicine three times a day," Maddie said. "And he's so fussy. I'd feel better keeping an eye on him. But thanks, anyway. I appreciate the offer."

While she was thanking Mrs. Johnston, Michael went to change Timmy and tuck him in for a nap.

"There are only a couple of diapers left," he said when he walked into the kitchen. Maddie was trying to swallow a couple of aspirin.

"I'd better pick up some disposable ones," Maddie said after she got them down. "In a moment of sheer madness I promised my cousin Linda on the phone that I'd keep Timmy until Friday. She's still trying to patch things up with her husband."

Michael leaned against the wall. "You'll do fine with Timmy." He smiled. "Silence. Beautiful silence. I bet he's already out like a light."

Maddie grinned. "Let's hope he sleeps for a few hours."

Michael pushed away from the wall. "Did you eat anything this morning?"

Maddie shook her head.

"Go sit down in the living room, and I'll put on some coffee and toast."

He reached out to steady her as she stumbled a little. Without a word she leaned against him. She could feel the muscles in his shoulder flex, smell the freshness of his heathery tweed jacket. He pressed his hand against her back, and a feeling of expectation suddenly arced through her body.

Michael tilted her head back as he studied her face. His hands slid over her silk dress.

They swayed, as though dancing to a very slow tune. Michael's gaze didn't waver from her face. *Why don't I pull her closer still? Let the warmth of her body heat me? Move my hands along the glorious lines of her face, her body? Slip that silky dress off her?*

The same feeling of urgency that filled Michael filled Maddie—and frightened her. *This is crazy, reckless,* she told herself. *And I'm never reckless. I'm not good at this sort of thing. I don't know what I'm doing. I'm jumping into the deep end of the pool, and I can't swim to save myself.*

She felt his mouth against her throat. She closed her eyes, giving herself over to a feeling that was both sharp and sweet.

He drew her back a little. She opened her eyes, but her vision was a touch hazy.

"Maddie, we shouldn't start something we don't intend to finish."

His voice brought her vision back into focus. Her hand pressed against the front of his shirt, to steady her and give her a bit more distance.

She chose to misinterpret his meaning. "I almost forgot. You have a plane to catch. You shouldn't be bothering with my breakfast. You've done enough. And I'm really not very hungry." Maddie tried to keep her voice light, but all the while her mind was shouting, *Liar. You're starving. Ravenous. Why not let Michael feed your hunger? Why not let him draw you back into his arms, stroke you, caress you, make love to you?*

She shook her head as though she'd been speaking her thoughts. *Where can it go? Nowhere. I don't want it to go anywhere. Neither does Michael.*

She moved another step away, swaying slightly. "You'd better go. Your plane—"

"They run every hour."

"Michael." She paused and took a breath. "My life's been turned upside down this weekend. I keep trying to right it, but it…it isn't easy." She stared at him. "You don't make it easy."

"Neither do you," he admitted.

They stared at each other at length. Finally Maddie said, "I don't think we should start anything, Michael. I have my work. It's all I can handle. It's enough."

"Is it?"

"Isn't it for you?"

"Sometimes I'm lonely," he admitted. "Just like you."

Maddie didn't argue the point. "We're all lonely sometimes."

"The question is, what do we do about it?"

Maddie knew very well that Michael's question was not rhetorical. He was grinning boyishly, and Maddie felt a charge of excitement course through her. *Get a hold of yourself,* she chastised. *You can't just fall into the man's arms because you're suddenly feeling lonely and a little desperate for something you've managed to chase away all these years.*

"Maddie, you're a vibrant, beautiful, intelligent woman, and..."

"Stop it, Michael." Maddie laughed uncomfortably. "You'll give me a swelled head." She took a step back as she spoke.

Michael moved right along with her. "And I want you."

Of course she knew that's what he was thinking, but the actual words still caused a shock wave to run through her.

"It wouldn't work." Her voice was low and scared. "It would be complicated."

"Not if we don't make it complicated. Let's make it easy, Maddie. We're both strong, intelligent, realistic."

"It's dangerous," Maddie whispered. "I want to do business with you."

"You also want to make love with me."

"No." She hesitated. "Yes."

He smiled. "Good."

She backed up a few more steps. "No, it isn't good. I mean, even if it weren't complicated—and don't you dare say it's easy again—we have a professional relationship to uphold. Besides, I'm just not very good at this, Michael. I haven't been with a man for a long time. And when I was . . ." This was so damn hard. "I'm just not able to really let go. I get self-conscious. What I'm trying to tell you, Michael, is that I'd be a disappointment." She turned away. "This is so embarrassing. Don't you see, I've done nothing but make a fool of myself since we met. I've got to quit while I still have any vestige of dignity left."

He turned her around to face him, leaned toward her, brushing his lips against hers. "I wouldn't take you for a quitter, Maddie."

She looked at him with imploring eyes. "Michael, please . . . don't."

His mouth found hers again, this time covering her lips, his tongue forcing them open, probing the moist warmth of her mouth.

She felt a reckless, womanly excitement stir inside her even as she felt stricken by the excitement, like a young girl. Her knees were weak. Her heart was pounding.

"Look," he said softly, releasing her, "I've been fighting it, too. Arguments spinning in my head. My own fears, concerns, trepidations. But I want you, Maddie. And I'm tired of fighting it. And—" he drew her closer "—while I admit I do critical evaluations of my workers, I don't do the same with lovers. I want to make love to you, Maddie, not score your performance." A slow smile curved his lips. "You don't have to perform for me, Maddie. I'll take care of everything. Trust me."

If she had the right kind of style, she would have simply thrown her arms around Michael, wrapped her body around him, laughed throatily and said, "I'm all yours, darling." But she'd never had that kind of style.

He lowered his head to kiss her again, but she put out her hand. "No. Wait." She was desperately trying to rally.

But Michael had no intention of making that easy. Even as she held him at arm's length, his fingers found their way under the cuffs of her dress, sending shivers up her bare arms. She could feel her control slipping several notches. She could feel herself surrendering to his subtle ministrations, but her response was anything but subtle. She felt dizzy, hot, and her pulse raced.

Again he lowered his head, and this time, before she could protest again, his mouth was on hers, blocking her words, kissing her roughly, his tongue circling the inside of her mouth.

Maddie dissolved. She was melting, gripping the sleeves of Michael's jacket for support. His hands cupped her elbows as if he knew she'd sink to the floor in a heap if he didn't prop her up.

She leaned against him, and he slid one arm firmly around her narrow waist, his other hand stroking her face with just the tips of his fingers. Very softly.

Maddie expelled her breath in a little sigh. *Yes,* she thought, *just let it happen. Don't think. Don't do anything. Just let him take charge.*

But those very thoughts spinning in her mind distracted her, made her tense, self-conscious. Michael was holding her so tightly to him that he was crushing her arm against his chest. As she tried to wriggle it free, Michael laughed softly, relaxing his grip, guiding her arm around his neck. But she felt gangly, her whole body awkward as he swooped her up in his arms.

"Michael . . ."

He kissed her as he carried her down the hall. Before he made it to the door of her bedroom, he collided with the wall. He laughed, but Maddie was too nervous to laugh.

"Relax," he said softly as he let her down gently on the bed. "Just follow my lead."

Even though her tension mounted, her arousal, just at the prospect of making love with this strong, sensual, tender man, seemed to be melting her body from the inside out.

He stood over her. He slipped off his jacket, wiggled his tie loose and lifted it over his head. He started to unbutton his shirt.

"No," he whispered, "open your eyes. Watch me, Maddie."

Her lids fluttered open. She lifted her gaze to his face. Her eyes glistened. Michael could see a hint of emerald in them. Slowly she lowered her eyes and watched him undo each button of his shirt and then take it off. She had seen his bare chest the night before, but it had been different then.

Michael took greedy delight in watching her rising desire play across her face. He leaned on the bed with one knee and slid his hands down over the soft silk of her dress. Maddie moved slightly so that he could lift it off over her head. Yes, just as he had imagined, he thought with a smile as he unclasped her white, lacy bra to reveal the pale, silken skin of her breasts. He placed his hands lightly over them. The skin there was warm, her nipples already hard, and so sensitive that she uttered a little cry when he ran his thumbs over them.

She was sitting up and he gripped her shoulders, lowering her onto her back, her head on the pillow. Then he stood again, his hand moving to his belt. This time he didn't have to demand that Maddie watch him. Wide-eyed, entranced, she caught every movement he made.

He unfastened the buckle of his belt, undid the button of his trousers, lowered the zipper, his gaze moving from her face to her glorious breasts as her chest rose and fell with each quickened breath.

And then, just as he was about to slide his trousers over his hips, his expression turned thoughtful. "Maddie. You are on the pill, aren't you?"

She sat up like a shot. "No. I thought . . . You said . . . You told me you were going to take care of everything." She grabbed a pillow and pressed it against her chest. "We can't, Michael. I never bothered about the pill. I told you it's been a long time since . . ." She stared up at him. "I knew it. I warned you it wouldn't work. I feel so dumb. So . . . naked."

Michael smiled as he sat down next to her and yanked the pillow from her. "You look great naked."

"I don't suppose you have . . . anything on you."

His smile broadened. "You caught me unprepared. I feel so dumb. So . . . naked." Teasingly he thrust the pillow against his chest.

She pried the pillow away with little resistance from Michael. "You look good naked."

They both laughed, dispelling the discomfort they'd both been feeling.

"I think I noticed a drugstore just down the street," Michael said.

Maddie nodded.

He kissed her shoulder, then let his hands skim the sides of her breasts. She shivered.

"Don't move. Stay just as you are. I'll be right back." He zipped up his pants and pulled on his shirt as he spoke. He was just opening the door when she called his name.

He turned, fully expecting her to back out, desperately afraid the moment was going to slip away.

"What's the matter?" He hadn't meant to sound gruff, but he could hear the edge of disappointment in his voice.

There she was, sitting in the middle of the queen-size bed, her face flushed, her honey hair tousled, her beautiful bare breasts so delicious, so inviting. And there was so much more of her yet to discover, savor. *You can't do this to me, Maddie,* he thought. *I'm in too deep.*

"I just thought—" she smiled a smile that was at once innocent and erotic."—that since you're going to the drugstore anyway, you might pick up some Pampers."

He expelled a breath, only then realizing he'd been holding it in. "Pampers. Sure."

"Thanks."

He nodded. Then he started to turn, coming to a frozen stop as he heard his name again.

"You thought I was going to say we better forget it, didn't you?" Her smile was arresting.

"I'm so glad you didn't" was all he answered.

"Me, too," she whispered, falling back on the pillow in a most wanton pose. "Take my key. It's on the front-hall table."

He made it to the drugstore and back in record time, not able to dispel his worry that in his absence Maddie might have had some second thoughts. Michael, on the other hand, in his excitement, was way beyond any but the most heated thoughts.

Out of breath, he shrugged off his topcoat, and took off his shoes, and dropping the king-size box of Pampers on the hall table, hurried down the hall to Maddie's bedroom.

"I was a little chilly, so I crawled under the covers. Did you get everything?"

"I wasn't sure what size."

Maddie grinned. "Condoms?"

Michael laughed. "Pampers." He undid his shirt more rapidly than last time. "I bought a dozen."

"Pampers?"

He grinned. "Condoms."

"I think you're overestimating . . ."

"I just don't want to be caught unprepared again." He quickly shed the rest of his clothes and crawled under the covers beside her.

"Brrrr. You're cold."

"Only on the surface. Inside I'm burning, Maddie."

"Oh, Michael," she whispered, laying her head against his naked chest.

"I'm sorry for the delay, Maddie."

"It makes it all more real."

He looked down at her. "Is that bad or good?"

"Good," she murmured. "Very good. I want this to feel real, Michael. My few past flings were always couched in so much fantasy. Unfulfilled fantasy, if I'm going to be honest."

Maddie's admission struck a chord in Michael. Like Maddie, sex had never been real for him, either, but in a different way. It had always been more a physical than a deeply emotional experience. Not that he'd had all that many involvements himself. And not that he didn't care about the women he'd been involved with, so much as he'd been able to keep those feelings from spilling over into his real world. Maddie made that separation impossible. By all rights that realization should have scared the hell out of him. But at the moment he was far too caught up in the thrill of Maddie's unfolding passionate nature to ponder fears.

8

MADDIE HAD IMAGINED what Michael's body would feel like next to hers, but no fantasy came close to the sheer physical thrill of the real thing. The sensation of being pressed against his powerful, finely muscled frame while his cold fingers drifted down her neck, across her shoulders, caressing the sides of her breasts, drove Maddie wild. Her self-consciousness and worry about feeling awkward vanished. She felt wonderful.

It was only as Michael slowly edged the blanket down to her waist that Maddie's nervousness returned.

His eyes were fixed on her face, but as he started to lower his gaze, Maddie gripped the blanket and tried to tug it up over her again.

"Don't, Michael." Her voice sounded feeble.

"I want to look at you, Maddie," he said in a soft, slow way.

"I may not hold up under close scrutiny."

He lowered his head, his lips touching a taut nipple. Maddie held her breath. "Trust me," he murmured huskily against her breast. "You will."

Maddie let out a long, unsteady breath as she uncoiled her fingers from the blanket.

With his tongue Michael marked a whisper-soft trail downward over her stomach. He could feel the muscles beneath her silky skin tense, but he merely continued his maddeningly languorous exploration.

She could feel his fingers, still cool, against the heated flesh of her inner thigh. She could feel his mouth moving in intoxicating little circles across her stomach. The blanket no longer covered her body at all, and the sharp contrast of cold and warmth made her shiver. Her breath came unevenly. She squeezed her eyes shut.

"Maddie." His breath fanned her face.

"Mmm."

"Open your eyes."

She obeyed.

He smiled down at her. "You're beautiful, Maddie. Every inch. Every flawless inch."

"Oh, Michael." She let her gaze run all the way down to his feet. "You're beautiful, too."

They both laughed softly, and then his mouth locked with hers. She gripped his shoulders, her fingers digging into his corded muscles. Maddie loved the way Michael kissed her. He was so intent, so absorbed. So thorough. His mouth, his tongue, his lips were intoxicating. She could feel herself letting go, no longer trying to fight it. No longer wanting to. She wanted him to go on kissing her forever. She wanted to feel the weight of his body on her forever. In total abandon she reached down in between them and caught gentle hold of him, stroking.

When a low moan escaped his lips, Maddie thought it was one of pleasure. Only when he stopped abruptly with another moan, this one more clearly a grunt, did Maddie freeze, unaware until that instant that her body had been moving involuntarily in an instinctive rhythm of desire.

He rolled off her. The sudden separation sent a chill through her. She opened her eyes, confusion, embarrassment, unmasked desire in her expression as she stared up at Michael, whose own visage was caught between a smile and a grimace.

"What's wrong? Is it me? Did I hurt you? Did I do something you didn't like? I know . . . I'm a little tense. It's just . . ." She sighed wearily. "I'm trying, Michael. I knew this was a bad idea."

"Maddie." The smile won out.

She stared up at him wanly. "Yes?"

He leaned lower. His mouth moved to her ear. "I found your brooch. Or to be more accurate, my big toe found it."

"What?"

Michael sat up, reached down toward the end of the bed between the mattress and the wall and retrieved the brooch.

"Oh, Michael." She sat up beside him, watching as he closed what proved to be a faulty clasp and placed it in the palm of her hand.

"It must have landed there when I was flinging the covers back looking for it. Are you hurt? Let me see."

He grinned. "Only if you promise to kiss it better."

"Don't tease. Not now. The Fates really do have it in for me, I swear." She stared ruefully down at the brooch.

Michael took it back and set it on the bedside table. Then he cupped her shoulders and eased her back into a reclining position. He kissed her lips very gently. "This is fate, too, Maddie." He kissed her again, still tender but more demanding.

When he sought her lips this time, he plunged his tongue deep into her mouth, retreated, plunged again. His kisses were relentless, exploring her mouth in a tortuous rhythm that made her move involuntarily in accompaniment to his insistent onslaught.

There was nothing languorous about Michael's seduction now. His strong, sinewy body moved on top of her, his weight forcing the air from her lungs so that she let out a low gasp. He caught hold of her wrists and stretched her arms over her head against the pillows. The movement made her back arch, her high, firm breasts thrust harder against his chest. He was all heat now. Heat and fire.

Still holding her pinned, he gazed down at her. His dark eyes were so bright they glistened. Maddie stared up at him, mesmerized. When he lowered his mouth to hers, they kissed in a timeless moment, capturing each other's breath.

Maddie's mind shut down, instinct and desire her only guide as her body moved beneath Michael's in an insinuating way. She thrilled to the rapid rise and fall of his chest and abdomen as he quickly matched her rhythm, and they breathed in unison.

When Michael released her wrists, her hands moved greedily down over the hard, satiny skin of his back. He shifted, his strong, muscular legs entwining her. This time she sought his lips, her tongue eager to explore his mouth. Her insides were turning to liquid as her hands grew bolder, moving down over his firm buttocks, pressing him more tightly to her.

Her hips moved against his. She ached to feel him inside her. She cried out his name. A fierce, restless yearning inflamed her. Boldly she stroked him, probing, caressing, thrilling to the erotic intoxication of their mingled gasps of pleasure. She felt his heat suffusing her.

"Oh, Michael, please..." she moaned against his neck.

He lifted his head slightly, looked down at her, saw the fierce desire in her features. "Fate, Maddie." And then, after a brief pause and the rustle of foil, he plunged deep into the core of her. Maddie gasped, her head thrown back. His lips came down onto her neck, sucking there until she moaned with pleasure.

As his movements quickened, she writhed beneath him, never once allowing him to slow. Each scorching stroke merged them closer together until she was suspended in a sublime, precious ecstasy, trembling like a leaf, crying out his name with abandon. And all the while he made his claim on her.

He wanted to keep watching the play of pleasure on her face, but his fleeting control made him shut his eyes, letting himself get lost in a blur of time and space. He wanted to slow down, prolong the moment, but he'd moved beyond that possibility. His desire was like a tidal wave, washing over his body, sweeping into his head.

Feverishly he sought her lips at the very moment of release. He groaned deep into her mouth. Maddie felt her whole body quiver and then her own release came in a helpless, uncontrollable explosion of sheer pleasure that flooded her entire body.

She clung to him for long moments afterward, aware of herself and Michael only, linked by the ecstasy they had shared so completely. She could still feel the ripples of pleasure spreading through her.

"I've never done this before, you know."

Michael grinned. "You could have fooled me." He turned onto his side to face her, a tender smile softening his angular features, his dark eyes surveying her warmly.

"I mean I've never made love in the afternoon before. It feels . . . more wanton somehow."

"Just think what you might have missed," he said in a teasing tone that, while tender, reminded Maddie that in so many ways they were still strangers. A flash of guilt and nervousness overtook her. She started to reach for the covers.

"Don't," Michael said softly.

"It's chilly."

"Maddie," he said firmly, cupping her chin, "making love in the afternoon with you was wonderful. It was the best afternoon I can remember spending."

"But not the wisest," Maddie said. "For either one of us." She gave him a worried look. "What happens now, Michael? How do we put aside what happened and ever get down to business?"

Michael stared at her in silence for a long moment. "Listen, Maddie. I told you that we're considering another company. But putting that aside for now, I've got this new idea ticking away in my head about Sargent. It could prove to be a better deal all around. I'm going to need a little time to pursue it, though. I think we'll be able to work it all out, Maddie. Just as long as we don't put any undue pressure on each other."

Maddie wasn't sure if Michael was talking about their personal relationship or their professional one. She had the feeling, however, that he probably meant both. She was also very uneasy about this new idea of his.

"What new idea?" she asked warily.

"I'll tell you all about it as soon as details are firmer."

Maddie eyed him with a stubborn expression. "I'd just as soon push for the old deal, Michael. You know the saying, 'A bird in the hand . . .'" She frowned. "Look, if you really decide some other company is better, I don't need you to throw a few crumbs my way as compensation," she said angrily.

"I'm not talking crumbs here, Maddie." He sighed in frustration. No point in trying to convince her until he could show her something concrete and, he hoped, exonerate himself.

"How about if we go out and get something to eat?" Michael suggested.

"You have a frustrating habit of switching topics when it suits your purposes, Michael."

He smiled. "How do you think I made it to the top?"

She sighed. "Okay. I guess I am hungry. But what about Timmy?"

"We won't be away for more than an hour. I think it would be fine to leave him with Mrs. Johnston for that long, if she's still available."

"I'll go shower and then call her," she said, unaware of the controlled sound of her own voice but fully aware of the self-consciousness that she experienced, rising naked from the bed.

She didn't need to look at him to know that he was watching her closely. She hurried over to the closet, grabbed her robe, put it on and headed quickly for the bathroom.

She was just stepping into the shower when the bathroom door opened.

"Mind if I join you?"

"Join me?" She felt herself flush.

He was standing there naked. It had been one thing to lie beside his naked body in bed in the throes of passion, but it was quite another to find herself, just as naked, standing across from him under a bright fluorescent bathroom light.

He was smiling, which only heightened her discomfort.

"I bet this is something else you've never done."

"Michael . . ."

His smile deepened. "You've been around a little, though, Maddie. You must have heard the saying, 'One hand washes the other.'"

"Michael." This time her voice was sharp, indignant. If he thought . . .

"I'm teasing you, Maddie. Don't you know when I'm teasing and when I'm serious?" He took a few steps into the bathroom and shut the door. "You really think that's what I'm like?"

Slowly she shook her head. She was unable to keep her eyes from traveling down his tanned, lean yet muscular body.

The tiny room was growing smaller as he approached. He paused less than a foot from her, staring at her, not at all uneasy in his nudity.

She held her breath, then closed the gap. The feel of his body against hers was an aphrodisiac. He drew her tight for a moment, then reached past her and turned the shower on. "How hot do you like it?" he murmured against her ear.

Maddie's insides were already molten. "Very hot" was her husky answer.

They stepped into the shower and stood together under the pulsing jets, smoothing soap all over each other and then kissing, clinging in a slippery embrace. He lathered her hair, giving her scalp a fantastic massage, and kissed her while the water rinsed the lather off.

She gasped as he pressed her against the cold tiles of the shower, the contrast with the heated water and their heated bodies almost intolerably erotic. She could feel him hard, demanding, between her soapy thighs.

He lifted her up, gripping her buttocks, locking her legs around his hips. They made love with the water jetting down over them.

Afterward, as he toweled her off, she smiled. "You're right. I never did take a shower with a man before." A little laugh escaped her lips. "It was an exceptional experience."

He encircled her in the towel and pressed her to him, giving her a loud, greedy kiss.

Maddie wrapped her arms around his neck. It was impossible to believe so much had happened between them so quickly. But it didn't feel as though she had passed through ordinary time these past few days. No, it had all been quite extraordinary. She buried her face against his still-damp neck, her fingers skimming down his back. His body dazzled her. He was so strong, so powerful, so responsive. And so tender and loving.

He lifted her head, his gaze capturing hers, blinding her to everything else. His lips found hers, their tongues making electric contact. Yes, quite extraordinary, she thought happily. As for the personal and professional complications, this wasn't the time to talk of them or even to think about them.

They returned to Maddie's bedroom and dressed in an easy, unhurried fashion. Then Maddie phoned Mrs. Johnston, who said she'd be happy to watch Timmy.

Timmy seemed in better spirits, and Maddie guessed that the antibiotics were already working. She was relieved to hand a cheerful baby into Mrs. Johnston's care.

Conscious of not wanting to leave Timmy for too long, Maddie chose a steak house a couple of blocks

from her place. They were both ravenous and chose
king-size portions of T-bone steak, with french fries and
salad, which they ate with relish.

Afterward they shared a hot-fudge sundae and finished off the bottle of Chianti Michael had ordered with
lunch.

"That was terrific." Maddie sighed, after the last
swallow of wine.

"I hope that covers more than the meal."

She grinned. "It does."

She watched him polish off the last of the sundae and
then leaned forward a little. "Michael, I know you were
teasing before about one hand washing the other, but I
am concerned that what happened this afternoon won't
influence your decision. Don't get me wrong. I want
that account desperately."

"Maddie—"

"Oh, I know, you're still considering all your op-
tions. I just want you to know that I don't expect any
favors."

The warmth and comfort Michael had been feeling
vanished. "Maddie, believe me, there won't be anything personal in my decision. I don't do business that
way. Ever." His tone was emphatic—perhaps to convince himself, even more than Maddie, that he couldn't
allow his personal feelings to interfere with his business judgment, now more than ever. Even so, he found
himself once again questioning whether he'd moved too
quickly on the L'Amour deal, only to conclude that he
knew damn well that it was the right company for the
new Barrett's line. But he really did have a terrific new
idea for Sargent. And if it panned out, he was sure
Maddie would be thrilled. If it didn't pan out . . .

Maddie saw Michael's features darken. She reached across the table and placed her hand on top of his. "One more thing, Michael. If you're worried that I have any expectations—business dealings aside—you can relax. No strings, Michael. No strings, no obligations, no claims." Her smile was soft and far more vulnerable than she realized. "Agreed?"

He exhaled a little raggedly. "Agreed."

But when they walked back in the biting cold to Maddie's apartment, Michael was very quiet and seemed lost in his own thoughts. She wondered if he was still planning to fly back to New York, but she didn't want to ask. The truth was, she didn't want him to go. What she wanted was to crawl back into bed with him. If she was going to be liberated enough for a no-strings-attached fling, why not have it last just awhile longer?

But Michael had other pressing issues on his mind. He checked his watch. It was nearly three. He wanted to place a call to Barrett and toss around this new idea that was becoming more pressing. If the old man bit, he'd fly to New York so he could set some more wheels in motion first thing in the morning. With any luck he'd be back in Boston in time for his sister's wedding rehearsal and dinner on Friday night. And he'd be able to come clean with Maddie and sweeten her disappointment at the same time.

Lost in his own thoughts, he didn't hear what Maddie was saying.

"Sorry," he apologized. "I wasn't listening."

"Nothing important. I just remembered when we passed the cleaners that they owe me for ruining a new dress of mine."

"Oh." He nodded.

Maddie smiled halfheartedly, trying not to feel rejected. They were in front of her building.

"Will you come up?"

"No," Michael said. "I can't. I've got some calls to make. And I still plan to fly back to New York."

No strings, she reminded herself. Michael was merely emphasizing the point. It was, she went on silently, unfair to set the terms and then feel miserable when they were carried out.

"New York. Right. I almost forgot. You were heading there this morning. I really did throw you off schedule, didn't I?" She couldn't look at him, so she focused her attention on his hands. He wasn't wearing gloves, and he hadn't stuck his hands in his pockets for warmth. They were handsome hands, strong yet capable of such tenderness. She could feel them caressing her body.

A warm smile softened the tense lines in his face. "It was a wonderful detour."

Maddie didn't smile back. "What about the dinner with all your relatives Tuesday night?"

Michael shrugged. "I'll grab a shuttle in for the evening, if I can. Then fly back to New York afterward." He paused. "I still owe you a dinner."

"You still owe me a business meeting," Maddie corrected.

"We'll have it. How about if I come down to your plant on Friday? You can show me around. And we can talk."

"All right." She was getting cold standing still. "I guess I'd better go relieve Mrs. Johnston."

"Oh, Maddie, I almost forgot. Do you have another tube of that skin cream you used on Timmy? I'd like to add it to the product-line samples you sent us."

Maddie brightened, thinking Michael had abandoned that new idea for Sargent he'd brought up before. "You like the idea of including it, then. That's great, Michael. It could be part of a five-step facial program. It would fit perfectly with the cleanser, toner and mineral masque I already sent you. Plus there's a new facial spray we're working on in conjunction with the moisturizer. As soon as I get into work tomorrow, I'll get one off to you. Or we could even zip down there now."

"Slow down, Maddie. Let's take it one step at a time. I'll just come up with you and get the tube of skin cream for now."

Maddie smiled. "Right." Michael followed her into the building. As they waited for the elevator, Maddie couldn't resist adding one more idea. "What about a special travel kit for the collection? In Barrett's colors. Silver background with a print of Bs in maroon? We could use one of our designers, or if you'd rather use someone at your end..."

"The elevator."

Impatiently Michael ushered Maddie inside and stepped in behind her. He didn't want to think about how he was going to feel on Friday afternoon if his new idea didn't pan out.

BEFORE HEADING OUT to the airport, Michael made a call to his boss from Barrett's Boston store only to learn that Barrett would be out of town until Wednesday. He hung up, drumming his fingers on the desk of the store manager who had discreetly gone off to attend to other matters. After a few minutes he placed another call to Joel Epstein, a manufacturer who was one of Barrett's biggest suppliers. He spent thirty minutes on the phone, ending the conversation by setting up a meeting at Epstein's office on Thursday morning. When he hung up this time, he was feeling a little better. Epstein was a shrewd businessman, and he hadn't built his reputation or his bank account by being overly cautious. He had a knack for getting into the right markets at the right time. He was willing to take risks as long as he believed the odds were in his favor. Michael was banking on being able to convince him this time around.

When he left the Barrett's store, Michael encountered rush-hour traffic on his way to the airport. Sitting in traffic gave him some time to reflect on everything that had happened during the past few days. He couldn't get Maddie off his mind. When he found himself waiting to board his plane, he considered calling her but vetoed the idea quickly. No, he needed to get some distance from Maddie. Their relationship had gained momentum all too quickly. She had bowled him over. Confused him. He couldn't sort out how he felt. But he was clear enough to know that his feelings weren't casual. And he knew Maddie's weren't, either. She'd said no strings. And he believed she meant it. She wasn't playing it cool in some reverse psychological ploy. Still, strings had a way of sneaking up on a person and catching one off guard. He flashed on that vision he'd had yesterday arriving with Maddie and Timmy at his mother's house. The happy little family. A cold chill shot through him.

In the end he gave his sister Cindy a ring, but he soon realized it had been a bad idea.

"Damn it, Cindy. Drop the subject."

"What did I say? All I said was that she's a nice woman. A warm, attractive, intuitive, sensitive, nice woman."

"Fine. She's all those things. I agree. Okay. She's warm, sensitive, beautiful. And if she were interested—which she isn't—she'd make some guy, some *other* guy, a terrific wife. Do I make myself clear?"

"You're absolutely right, Mike." Cindy laughed. "Beautiful is a better description than attractive."

THE NEXT MORNING Maddie deposited Timmy once again with Mrs. Johnston, who'd clearly developed a genuine affection for the baby and wouldn't hear of Maddie hiring a professional service to look after him. Maddie made it to work just as the morning meeting she'd scheduled was starting. Several times during the meeting with Liz and three other key staff people she'd had to ask people to repeat what they'd been saying. And with an embarrassed laugh she confessed that she hadn't had a chance to go over Larry Gibbon's last market report. All four stared at her with curious expressions. Reviewing the report had been the chief reason Maddie had called the meeting.

As the foursome switched gears, getting into their typical business-management discussions about targeting, strategy and new-product development, Maddie remained oddly distracted. Liz kept glancing over at her with a bemused expression, especially after receiving a vague response to her question about the status of the Barrett's account.

When the meeting was over, Liz followed Maddie uninvited into her boss's inner sanctum, a large, airy office with a trestle-table desk, a cozy seating group done in soft butter-cream velour in one corner and a bank of windows along the far wall that looked out onto the Charles River.

Maddie sat down at her desk and shot a quick glance up at Liz, who had shoved aside some papers and perched herself on a corner of the desk, facing Maddie.

"This is a first, Maddie."

Maddie looked alarmed. "What do you mean?"

"In almost seven years together, I have never seen you unprepared for a meeting. Especially since you told me you were staying home all day yesterday to catch up on work."

"Well—" Maddie swallowed hard "—it was a hectic day. With Timmy. Taking care of a baby is a lot of work, Liz. A lot of work. It's . . . distracting."

"Mm-hmm."

"What does that mean?"

Liz grinned. "Something tells me Timmy wasn't your only distraction."

Maddie's eyes widened. "How did you know?"

Liz winked. "Lucky guess."

"Oh."

"No, it's more than that. You've got the classic signs, Maddie."

"What classic signs? I don't know what you're talking about, Liz." Maddie ran her hand through her hair and sighed. "I didn't sleep well last night."

Liz chuckled. "That's one of them. I bet you skipped breakfast, too. Weren't hungry, right?"

Maddie looked chagrined. "Right."

Liz leaned closer. "And you can't think straight."

Maddie smiled sheepishly. "It's only temporary. It'll pass." Her smile faded. "I'm the last woman in the world for this to happen to."

"What's happening, Maddie?" Liz didn't need the answer for her confirmation but for Maddie's.

"It's . . . an infatuation. I'm going to put Michael Harrington out of my mind."

"Does that mean quitting negotiations on the Barrett's deal?"

"No," Maddie answered quickly. "Thank God, Michael is a professional. Our business dealings are a separate issue."

"Then you won't exactly be able to put Michael out of your mind."

"You know what I mean, Liz," Maddie said impatiently, grabbing a pen and making little nervous doodles on a sheet of paper.

When Liz didn't say anything, Maddie dropped the pen and looked up at her. Her whole body ached from fatigue. She'd tossed and turned all night, unable to find a comfortable position, her bed never feeling wider or emptier. Ever since Michael had taken off yesterday, she hadn't been able to think about anything but him, her body in a frustrating state of semiarousal. But worse than the state of her body was the state of her mind. She had always been so clear-thinking, so sure of who she was, what she wanted, what she needed—and didn't need. She was sensible, independent, her own person. She'd spent practically her whole life alone. She'd never been really intimate—physically or emotionally—with anyone. Those few times she'd made a stab at closeness with Felicity had been awkward, embarrassing, ultimately disastrous.

But this weekend with Michael . . . she'd felt closer to him than she'd ever felt to anyone. Michael had transformed her awkwardness into abandon. He'd made her feel vibrant, alive. Michael made her imagine another world, a world of waking each morning with him, sitting across from him at the breakfast table, even taking turns making the bottle and feeding their own baby, singing little lullabies together. . . .

Maddie gripped her abdomen. "My stomach feels jumpy."

Liz laughed softly. "That's one of the classic signs, too."

9

MADDIE ARRIVED at Mrs. Johnston's door after work feeling chilled, frazzled and out of breath.

Mrs. Johnston insisted that she come in for a hot cup of tea. Maddie agreed out of gratitude, but she would have much preferred to go straight upstairs with Timmy, settle him for the night, take a hot shower and crawl into bed. It had been a tough day at work. She'd felt disorganized, disoriented, unable to concentrate. And her conversation with Liz had only made her more distracted.

While Maddie stepped out of her boots and slipped off her coat, Mrs. Johnston went to get Timmy, who was resting in the crib Mrs. Johnston kept for her granddaughter. As soon as Timmy saw Maddie, his face broke out in a big smile, his plump little arms stretching out in her direction. Maddie felt a rush of pleasure, and when she took him in her arms and he nuzzled her contentedly, she laughed.

"Hi, Scout. Looks like you had a nice, peaceful day." Which was more than she could say for herself.

Maddie followed Mrs. Johnston to the kitchen and sat at the table while she put on the kettle for tea.

"I really appreciate you watching Timmy while I was at work today, but I can't tie up your whole week, Mrs. Johnston. I should try to track down a baby-sitter."

"Nonsense. I wouldn't hear of it. I love looking after Timmy. He's an angel." Mrs. Johnston smiled as she looked over at the baby, who was busily playing with Maddie's hair. "He missed you today."

"No." The notion seemed impossible to Maddie.

"Oh, he did. You should have seen his face light up when I put him next to the telephone when you called me this afternoon to check on him."

"He did?" Maddie tenderly stroked Timmy's back. And then she flushed. "I wasn't checking on him. I knew you were taking wonderful care of him. I just..." Maddie wasn't really sure why she had called. Or why she, too, had brightened when she heard Timmy's soft cooing into the receiver.

"You just missed him," Mrs. Johnston said. "We get attached to babies so quickly. That's the way it should be. Hold a little bundle of joy in our arms and we all melt."

Maddie smiled down at Timmy. "Well, he is a sweet baby. As babies go, I mean."

"They're all sweet. Even the fussy ones. When you have your own, you'll see."

"No. Not me. Babies aren't in my plans. It's too hard to juggle a busy career and a family at the same time. I'm not looking for the superwoman award of the year," Maddie added emphatically.

"You just need a husband who'll pitch in. Plenty of men are doing it. My son-in-law, Garry, helps my daughter out all the time. She's a teacher and she went back to work when the baby was eight months old. She and Garry take turns getting up early to feed the baby and get her dressed. Garry changes her diapers and takes her to the doctor at the first sign of a sniffle. Half the time he's the one the baby-sitter calls when there's a problem with Jennifer."

Maddie couldn't help thinking, as Mrs. Johnston went on raving about her son-in-law, that Michael would be that kind of father—caring, attentive, involved. Not, she told herself quickly, that that was relevant. Michael might be a wiz with kids, but he didn't want any of his own any more than she did.

They drank their tea, and Maddie switched the conversation to more mundane chatter. Meanwhile Timmy munched contentedly on a teething cookie, although he was adamant about remaining in Maddie's lap, fussing each time she tried to set him in the small feeding seat Mrs. Johnston kept on hand for her granddaughter's visits. Maddie was certainly not going to admit it, but she felt a growing pleasure that Timmy was becoming attached to her. For a pair who'd started off on the wrong foot, they'd come a long way. That thought instantly led her to thoughts of Michael. Talk about starting off on the wrong foot. Talk about having come a long way. Unfortunately, she took little pleasure in that realization. She'd spent half the day at work chastising herself for her impetuous involvement with Michael, the other half fighting to make sense of her confused feelings.

On her way up to her own apartment fifteen minutes later, Maddie once again thought about her conversation with Liz that morning. Was her assistant right? Did she have the classic signs of a woman in love? It wasn't possible. It couldn't be possible. In love with Michael? After such a short time? It was ridiculous. Liz didn't think there was anything so astonishing about it, though. If love at first sight had become a cliché, she'd said, it must be because it had happened enough times to become one.

"Love at first sight," Maddie muttered aloud as she unlocked the door and stepped into her apartment. "Nonsense. It's merely an infatuation."

Timmy looked up at her, his cherubic face bearing a broad smile. Maddie found that smile surprisingly intimidating.

"Oh, so you don't believe me."

Timmy giggled.

"Well, Scout, it's true. And, I might add, a passing infatuation. And the same is true for Michael. Just look at the way he scooted out of here yesterday. I bet right this minute he's sorely regretting..." She stopped, gave Timmy a shrewd smile. "Well, never you mind what he's regretting. How about we change the subject? Let's talk about dinner. Cream of rice for you and a hamburger for me. What do you say?"

Timmy gave her a look that seemed to say he found the talk about her and Michael more interesting.

Maddie grimaced. "I don't know, Tim. I truly must be off my rocker to be having a conversation with a six-month-old. I'm beginning to get a little worried about my state of mind."

With single-minded determination Maddie busied herself making dinner, feeding Timmy, giving him his bath and tucking him in for the night. Only after she pulled the blanket up over Timmy did it dawn on her that she'd gone about the tasks of child care with an absentminded ease. A slow smile curved her lips. *My, my,* she thought, *how much I've learned in such a short time.* And then, unbidden, came the thought, *How much Michael's taught me.*

The moment he snuck back into her mind, Maddie realized she'd lost the battle. She had to face it. Her senses were filled with thoughts of Michael. They exhausted her.

She decided to get to bed early, hoping sleep would come easier tonight, scared that if it didn't, it would only confirm one of Liz's classic signs. Those signs were beginning to take on a decidedly ominous cast for Maddie.

She undressed and went into the bathroom to shower. But as soon as she reached to turn on the water, she could see Michael reaching for the knob, asking in that low, sexy voice how hot she liked it.

Oh, God, she thought despairingly, *I must be in love. I can't even shower without him.* Tears filled her eyes.

Resolutely she decided on a bath, filling the tub with some bubble bath Felicity had brought her from Paris a few months ago.

Felicity. What would her mother make of her daughter's state of mind? Not for the first time Maddie found herself wishing she had the kind of mother she could confide in. She felt an urgent longing to be able to phone her mother, tell her to come over and help her sort out her confused feelings. She wanted motherly advice. She wanted a warm, nurturing caress, a gentle pat, a mother's understanding, knowing smile.

Fat chance she'd get that from the urbane Felicity, even if she could track her down. And if she were to confide in her mother, Felicity would no doubt give her a wry smile and tell her she was taking the whole matter far too seriously. Her advice would be to stick Michael in a tidy little cubbyhole, and if he became too bothersome, to cut him loose and go off and buy a new dress. For Felicity, love was carefree, unencumbered. She had certainly never let her personal relationships get too involved or allowed them to pull her off her own fast track. Maddie recalled that last postcard she'd received from Felicity, the one Michael had read.

"Well, Mom, I didn't have to fly off to Greece with you to find the man of my dreams. He walked right in my front door. I hope you're satisfied."

She sank deeper into the hot water, drawing her knees up to her chest, wriggling her toes among the bubbles. The fragrant, soapy heat was disturbingly sensual. Maddie closed her eyes, resting her chin on her wet knees. She wished she could take the advice Felicity would give. She wished she could be more detached, more casual about what had happened between her and Michael. She was angry at herself for falling in love so quickly, so impetuously.

She had to be very careful to keep her feelings under wraps. Michael must never know. Seen through his eyes, her feelings would appear traitorous. She was supposed to be a plucky lass with the same perspective on life and love as Michael. That was what he found so appealing about her. She wasn't threatening. She wasn't waiting with bated breath to snare him.

What was the matter with her? They'd made love together once—twice, she amended—and already she was thinking she wanted to marry him.

She stiffened. Who said anything about marriage? She looked around the bathroom in an absurd belief that some invisible being had heard her thoughts and would hold her to them.

Her panic gave way to relief. Nonsense. So she'd let herself get temporarily carried away by a few idle fantasies about Michael. Fantasies were a far cry from reality. She just wasn't used to them. She mustn't let herself dwell on them. She told herself that they were under her control. They were her secret. Thank God she hadn't said anything to Michael about being in love with him. No, she'd handled things very well. Nothing to feel awkward about. Nothing to worry about. She hadn't jeopardized anything. She felt confident she still had a clear shot at getting the contract for that exclusive line with Barrett's. Even more than before. After all, Michael had even taken along that new moisturizer gel with him.

She stepped out of the tub, vowing once again to put Michael out of her mind. Of course, no sooner had she made the vow than she thought about him, this time surrounded by his family and relatives. Tonight was the big gathering at one of the local restaurants for his out-of-town relatives in for the wedding.

At the thought of that loud, gay get-together, Maddie felt a sudden intense loneliness and had to squeeze her eyes shut to stop the flow of tears. Her feelings angered her. Until Michael came along, she'd been perfectly content in her aloneness. Until Michael came along, she'd been undisturbed by fantasies of marriage, of having a baby. How dare he, she fumed, walk into her life and send it into such a complete turmoil?

The anger was refreshing. Maddie held on to it as she crawled into bed. It was only a little after nine o'clock, but Maddie was determined to get a good night's sleep. So much for Liz's classic signs! She flicked off the light, pulled the covers up over her head and shut her eyes.

Ten minutes later she flung the covers off. Timmy's antibiotic. She'd forgotten about his last dose. Damn.

She tiptoed into the spare bedroom. Timmy was sound asleep. Now what? Should she wake him and give him his medicine? Should she skip it tonight and give him a double dose in the morning? Was it too late to call Mrs. Johnston and ask her advice? What would

Michael do? *I can't think straight. I'm not any good at this.*

The sound of the doorbell startled her and woke Timmy up. He started to cry. Maddie sniffed back tears, picked up Timmy and went to see who was there.

Her heart turned over as she looked through the peephole and then opened the door. "Michael."

Seeing her red eyes and Timmy's tear-drenched face, Michael's brow creased. "Maddie, what is it?"

She smiled and sniffed at the same time. "I forgot to give Timmy his last dose of medicine. And then he was asleep, and I didn't know if I should wake him."

A tender smile curved Michael's lips. "Well, he's up now." He walked in and shut the door. "Where's his medicine?"

Maddie laughed. "Oh, Michael, you've done it again. You've saved the day."

He put his arm around her and Timmy. "Think nothing of it."

But of course that wasn't possible, given Maddie's state of mind.

After Timmy had swallowed his medicine and Maddie had tucked him back into bed, she returned to the kitchen to find Michael putting on coffee.

Maddie stood watching him. "I thought you were at a dinner with your out-of-town relatives tonight."

"I was." He plugged in the coffee and turned around to her. "My family was disappointed that I didn't bring you along."

Maddie smiled awkwardly. "I guess they still have the wrong idea."

Michael's smile was just as awkward. "I guess so."

They stood a few feet apart. Their eyes met and held.

"Why did you come here?" she asked finally, her voice weak.

He didn't answer immediately, but his gaze grew more intense. "I missed you," he admitted.

He hesitated for a moment and then, bridging the gap between them, cupped her face gently in his hands.

Maddie trembled at his touch. "I missed you, Michael."

He smiled for an instant at her words, and then he sobered. His eyes locked on hers. "We do have an understanding, Maddie. We do see things alike. No marriage. No family. No promises. We can handle this—don't you think?"

Maddie nodded silently, unaware that she'd lowered her eyes.

He tilted her head up and kissed her lips very gently. "I do want you, Maddie. I have never wanted any woman the way I want you."

She leaned into him, returning his kiss. She felt exhilarated and sad at the same time. As if from a distance she heard herself say, "I want you, too, Michael."

He kissed her again, this time more roughly and more possessively. She tensed at first, a reflexive response.

"Let go, Maddie," he whispered against her well-kissed lips. "I want to make love to you. Right here. Right now."

He opened her robe and drew her flannel nightgown up, kissing her breasts, her nipples growing hard beneath his lips. He gripped her hands tightly, drawing them behind her back, entwining his fingers with hers.

Maddie could feel an extraordinary tension emanating from her body. The fierce intensity of her own longing coupled with Michael's frightened her and excited her at the same time. She kissed him on the mouth, a hard, frenzied kiss.

Michael could feel her trembling race through her muscles. He released her hands, tugged off her robe, lifted her nightgown over her head. Then he pulled her to him, flattening her against his length with such force that she gasped.

The contrast between her nakedness and his fully clothed body flooded Maddie with a sexual wildness. She wound her arms around him possessively, her fingers pressing into the contours of his muscles. She could feel the outline of him, hard and hot, beneath the barrier of his trousers.

As Michael hoisted her up, her feet no longer touching the floor, and pressed her against the counter, a recklessness consumed her. She felt heat suffuse her as she stripped off his shirt, then snaked her hand down to free him from the confines of his trousers.

Michael's breath caught, then came in jagged, fiery exhalations as her hand engulfed him. He had never felt so aroused. He could feel his whole body quivering, his buttocks clenched tightly as he pushed up hard against her, frantic for union.

"Now," she said to him. "Yes, now." Her voice, husky with lust, filled Michael with promises of unsurpassed delight. A brief pause for a condom and then he penetrated her in one long, heated slide.

"Oh, Michael." Maddie clenched him fiercely, rhythmically, and she burned with passion, exquisitely joined to him. Her head went back, her eyelids fluttering, and she let go completely, Michael supporting her. Release burst inside of her, bringing her indescribable joy. She sighed with it, pleasure and ecstasy combining, filling her with a contentment unlike any she had ever known.

For Michael, release came as a surge of electricity, bringing with it deep, shuddering breaths. His fingers tangled in Maddie's hair as he brought his mouth to hers and they kissed long and hungrily, tongues caressing, lost within their shared ecstasy.

Later they made love again, more conventionally, but no less passionately, in Maddie's bed.

Maddie was half dozing when she felt Michael's weight shift away from her. She flung her arm out. "Don't go."

His hand moved caressingly over her bare breast. "I wasn't leaving. I was just going to check on Timmy. I thought I heard him wake up."

Fully awake now, Maddie squinted at the glowing dial of her alarm clock. It was four in the morning. "You stay in bed. You've got a flight to catch in the morning."

Michael shook his head. "You've got to go to work in the morning. I'll go."

They laughed. Then Maddie snuggled against him. "Okay—" she yawned and stretched languorously "—you can go this time. I'll go next time."

He pinched her bottom. "You could have put up a bigger fight," he teased, shivering as he rose from the bed.

Maddie rolled onto her stomach. "I feel too good to fight."

A few minutes later Michael scooted back under the covers, and Maddie moved against him, nestling into him.

"He's asleep," Michael murmured. "I must have been wrong."

"Mmm, let me warm you," she whispered, draping a long, slender leg over him, and thinking how wonderful it was to have a strong, reassuring body to curl up to.

"Anytime," Michael answered, his palms sliding down the satin smoothness of her naked back.

Does he mean that? Maddie wondered. *Anytime?* And then her thoughts changed abruptly. *Get a hold of yourself. Don't start reading more into this than he meant.*

His mouth found hers. His tongue circled inside the moist depths, then slid along her teeth. He urged her on top of him. "Yes," he whispered, "Warm me, Maddie, Warm me."

She knelt over him, supporting herself on her outstretched arms. Her thick honey-blond hair trailed across his chest as she lowered her head and captured his lips. Then she pressed the entire length of her body against him, reaching down between his thighs, catching gentle hold of him, stroking him. All the while she kissed him deeply, greedily. Then after quickly attending to birth control, she helped guide him inside her and began moving rhythmically, Michael matching her movements.

Oh, Michael, she thought, *I love you. I ache with love. I want to warm you. I want to go on warming you forever. How could I let this happen?*

Her fleeting despair vanished as she felt herself dissolving, melting, surrendering completely, currents of pleasure coursed down her spine.

The velvet darkness gave way to misty daylight before they fell asleep.

SURFACING RELUCTANTLY from a delightful dream-filled sleep, Maddie reached out for the alarm clock that was blaring. Michael, already out of bed, got to it before her.

"Sorry, I forgot to shut it off," he apologized. "I was going to let you sleep a little longer. I put on some fresh coffee, gave Timmy a bottle and took a shower."

She squinted at Michael, who was wearing only a towel wrapped around his waist and smiling down at her.

He looked wonderfully handsome, his dark hair damp, droplets of water still clinging to his broad chest. She rolled onto her stomach and pulled the covers up. "Don't look at me. I look a mess."

"Turn over." The side of the bed dipped as he sat beside her.

Slowly she moved onto her back. A muscle in his cheek moved, and his dark, intriguing eyes rested thoughtfully on her face. "You're beautiful in the morning, Maddie."

She smiled shyly.

He kissed the pulsating spot on her throat. "Do you know how long it's been since I made love to you?" His breath was hot against her skin, his damp hair sending a little shiver down her spine, a luxurious delight filling her.

But reason and practicality in the form of a baby's wail brought them both down to earth.

They looked at each other and grinned. "Ah, the joys of parenthood." Michael winked, pulling her up and pulling the covers off her at the same time. "Your turn, little mother."

His eyes traveled wickedly over the smooth curve of her breasts and hips and down the long, slender line of

her legs as she rose from the bed. He got a secret thrill
at the way she walked across the room this time for her
robe. Unlike before, she seemed completely comfortable in her nakedness. They were making progress.

He felt a surge of desire twist in him like a bittersweet pain. Just what kind of progress was he hoping
to make with Maddie? His brows knitted, his stomach
performed a sudden unpleasant flip. Why think of the
future at all? Maddie was quite content to take what
was happening between them in stride. There'd been no
weak moments during passion where she'd whispered
words of undying love. She enjoyed him, enjoyed their
lovemaking. She'd managed to keep the relationship in
perspective. He had to do the same. But in a moment
of complete honesty he admitted to himself that it was
going to be a most difficult thing to do.

FEELINGS OF GUILT, discomfort and worry might have
been floating around both Maddie and Michael's minds
that morning, but on the surface the scene in her kitchen
was one of pure domestic tranquility—Maddie, in her
robe and slippers, adeptly toweling Timmy off after his
bath in the kitchen sink; Michael barefoot, wearing his
trousers and shirt, but not having bothered to button
it, popping bread into the toaster; the radio tuned in to
a weather station; the announcer promising a clear,
crisp day.

"No problem getting to New York," Maddie said
lightly, slipping a disposable diaper under Timmy, who
was toying with one of the buttons on her robe.

"No. No problem."

She glanced over at the kitchen clock. "I should still
be able to make my meeting with our chief chemist. It's
not until ten."

"I can drop you off if you like."

"No, that won't be necessary. I should use my car. I think it stalled on me that night . . ." She smiled, remembering. "It stalls if I don't drive it every day."

"And conditions that night were rather . . . unusual."

Maddie's smile deepened for a moment. But then she busied herself finishing diapering Timmy.

Michael gingerly took out the steaming toast after it popped up and set the pieces down on a plate on the counter. "Butter or jam?"

"Butter." She picked up the diapered baby and turned with him to face Michael. "Well, what do you think? Not a bad job if I do say so myself."

Michael stopped buttering. "Terrific job. See that. It turns out you have a knack with babies, Miss Sargent."

"And no diaper rash, either, thanks to my wonder cream."

He walked over and kissed her cheek. "Maybe you're in the wrong line."

Maddie gave him a bemused smile. "Don't tease, Michael. I'm very proud of our products. And women, nationwide, love them. You saw some of our endorsements in that packet I sent. And if Barrett's features our exclusive line, we're both going to be in clover, Michael."

She saw a muscle work at his jaw, and she had to remind herself that Michael had already made it clear that Sargent wasn't the only company being considered for the contract. And that he didn't want her to press him. It was obvious to Maddie by now that Michael was not completely sold on her line, which was exactly why she couldn't let the opportunity pass to plug it. She would have liked to get in a few more plugs, but the doorbell rang.

Maddie grabbed a baby blanket and threw it around Timmy as she hurried with him to the front door. "That must be Mrs. Johnston."

Maddie turned the knob, opened the door—and her mouth dropped open, though no words escaped.

"Darling . . ." That was all the marvelously tailored, attractively coiffed woman said before her glance slid down to Timmy and *her* mouth dropped open. But Felicity Sargent was not a woman left speechless for too long. "Where did you get him?"

Before Maddie could answer, Michael popped out of the kitchen and into the hall, spotted Felicity and quickly started to button his shirt.

"And *him*?" Felicity smiled coquettishly. She patted Maddie's cheek softly, her smile deepening. "And here I thought I was going to bend your ear with *my* adventures."

Maddie couldn't help laughing. "For once I topped you, Felicity." And then, Maddie's eyes sparkling, an impish grin on her face, she added, "Say hi to Timmy. He's your newest relative."

"Madeline." Beneath the perfectly applied makeup Felicity blanched.

"Why, Mother, you haven't called me Madeline in years."

Felicity raised her eyebrows. "And you haven't called me Mother in years."

Maddie grinned. "A slip of the tongue."

Felicity watched Michael approach, eyeing him closely. "I suppose that means that he's a relative, too."

Michael put his arm around Maddie. "Hey, I thought I was the only tease in the family."

Felicity, not getting the joke, shook her head and brushed past the happy little threesome. "I think I need a drink."

"It's only eight in the morning," Maddie said, trying to contain a burst of laughter.

"I'm still functioning on European time." Felicity pulled off her Italian leather gloves, undid her black cashmere coat and flung them both on the couch, draping herself carelessly over them. "All right. I'll settle for coffee."

"Let me," Michael offered.

"Thanks, dear." Maddie winked.

Felicity narrowed her gaze. "When did all this happen?"

Maddie grinned. "Sometimes it feels like forever."

"How old is that baby, Maddie?"

"Timmy? Six months. Here, why don't you hold him."

"Wait a minute, Maddie," she muttered as her daughter placed the blanketed baby in her arms.

"He likes you, Felicity. He usually screams bloody murder when he's dumped into a stranger's arms. I guess he must sense that you're family."

A sheen of perspiration broke out across Felicity's brow. She looked terribly awkward and uncomfortable holding Timmy, but the baby truly didn't seem to mind, his eyes fixed on the glistening white strand of pearls Felicity was wearing.

"This isn't possible," Felicity went on, her hazel eyes, a deeper shade than Maddie's, resting on Timmy as she did some mental arithmetic. "I haven't been gone that long. When did I see you last, Maddie? It can't have been more than eight or nine months, can it?"

Before Maddie could answer, Michael entered with a cup of coffee for Felicity. "Here, let me take Timmy and get him dressed." They made an exchange. All the while Felicity took in the scene with baffled amazement.

As Michael brushed past her with Timmy, Maddie couldn't hold back her mirth any longer. Laughing, she crossed the room and sank down next to Felicity on the couch. "Oh, it's really a crazy story."

Felicity stared at her daughter, a wry smile on her lips. "I can imagine. Why, I never dreamed..." She scrutinized Maddie closely. "You do look radiant, though."

Maddie's laughter faded, a soft flush rising in her cheeks. "I do?" And then she did something she hadn't done in more years than she could remember. She suddenly threw her arms around her mother and hugged her tightly. "I'm so glad to see you," she whispered, tears seeping out the corners of her eyes.

Felicity, taken aback, stiffened for a moment. And then she did something she, too, hadn't done in years. She smoothed back her daughter's hair and kissed her tenderly on her cheek. "I'm glad, too, darling."

Demurely Felicity Sargent dabbed at her eyes when her daughter released her.

10

"WHAT A DREADFUL THING to do. It's not like you to pull a prank like that, Maddie," Felicity said testily after Maddie explained the truth about Timmy's presence. As for the truth about Michael's presence, Maddie did not go into detail. Nor did Felicity press for any.

Maddie knew her mother was irritated by her little "prank," but she could also see the relief flooding Felicity's face. She felt a pang of disappointment, but not surprise at her mother's reaction. "Was the notion of being a grandmother that ghastly?"

Michael, sitting in an armchair with Timmy, observed mother and daughter thoughtfully. He had picked up Felicity's relief, too. But for a brief instant after Maddie's confession he could have sworn Felicity had cast Timmy a wistful glance. She'd regained her composure quickly, however, and Michael doubted Maddie had picked up that momentary flash of regret.

Felicity finished her second cup of coffee, set it down on the low glass-topped table and looked over at her daughter. "Well, darling, that kind of news does take some preparation. Why do you think nature gives us nine months?"

Maddie raised a brow. "I thought that was for the mother, not the grandmother. Anyway, you don't have to worry." Maddie shot a quick glance at Michael before looking back at her mother. "You won't have any little tykes running about calling you Nanny on my account."

Felicity smiled airily as she snapped open her purse and reached for a cigarette, rummaging around for her lighter. "You know my philosophy, Maddie. I've raised you to pursue any endeavor you so choose." She glanced at Timmy, a curious smile on her lips. "It's just that I never envisioned you as a mother, that's all." She gave up her search for her lighter and looked at Michael. "Do you have a light?"

Michael smiled pleasantly. "No, sorry. It's probably not such a good idea to smoke around the baby, anyway."

Felicity appeared a bit taken aback, but then she shrugged, setting her unlit cigarette on the coffee table beside her empty cup. "It has been ages since I've been around a baby." She smoothed back her short, stylishly coiffed, perfectly tinted blond hair. "I don't think I smoked when you were a baby, Maddie. I seem to recall it was that awful Rory Albertson who started me smoking about fifteen years ago. Do you recall him? A marvelous artist. I believe he was into mixed media when we first met."

Maddie couldn't recall him. But then, if Rory Albertson hadn't been around during her brief school vacations, it was unlikely Maddie would ever have learned of his existence.

Felicity hadn't bothered to wait for Maddie's response. "Such a talent, but really an impossible man. Self-destructive, I kept telling him. When I discover someone truly exceptional, I'll do everything in my power to bring him along. But Rory was terribly undisciplined, and he drank far too much. And carousing with his buddies...well, let me tell you, I had to bail him out of jail more than once. I finally came to my senses and realized that it was never going to work. If only he would have pulled himself together and fulfilled the contracts I'd lined up for him . . ."

Felicity sighed. "Oh, well, fortunately there haven't been too many Albertsons in my life. I'm afraid I was foolish enough to let myself get a little emotionally attached to him. It affected my usually astute judgment. I can thank Rory for one thing, though. He taught me that it's never a good idea to get personally involved with an artist you intend to represent."

Michael and Maddie shared an uncomfortable glance, both pulling their eyes away at the same time.

Felicity absently picked up her cigarette again and then, remembering, put it back down, muttering, "I should give them up, anyway."

The phone rang. Maddie rose from the couch and went to answer it. It was Mrs. Johnston on the line. In a very apologetic voice she explained to Maddie that she would not be able to watch Timmy today as planned, and very likely not for the rest of the week. A close friend, she hurriedly went on, had suddenly taken ill, and she had to go off to Newton, a suburb west of Boston, to take care of her.

"That's all right, Mrs. Johnston." Maddie made an effort to keep the disappointment from her voice. "I understand. You've been wonderful. I'll work something out. Don't worry. I hope your friend feels better."

"Problem?" Michael asked when Maddie hung up and turned back to face her mother as she spoke.

A panicked look flashed across Felicity's face. "Don't look at me, darling. I've got a thousand things to do while I'm in town. And I'm completely out of practice with babies, you know that."

Michael rose with Timmy from the chair. "I wish I could help, Maddie, but I've really got to get back to New York this morning. I've got several meetings...."

Maddie raised a hand to silence him. "Of course, Michael. I understand. You've rescued me more than enough times already." She crossed to Michael and took Timmy in her arms. "Maybe I'll take him to work. Between me and Liz we should be able to cope. I'd better finish getting ready."

Felicity stood, carefully smoothing out invisible wrinkles in her skirt. "Well, I should be going, too, darling. I was about to suggest lunch, but if you will be busy with the baby..."

"Timmy has to eat lunch, too, Felicity."

To her credit, Felicity laughed. "See. I told you it's been ages. Well, why don't we meet at Ricco's, then. I imagine they can dig up a high chair or some such thing for the baby."

Maddie smiled. The idea of sitting with her elegant, urbane mother at the posh little Italian café while Timmy strung spaghetti over his high chair as if it were a Christmas tree greatly amused her.

Laughing at the image, Maddie walked over to her mother. "I think we'd be better off at the Waldorf Cafeteria. Why don't you ring me at the office, and we'll make a final decision. Here, hold Timmy for a minute, will you?"

Felicity stepped back abruptly as if Maddie were passing her a grenade.

"He doesn't bite, I promise."

Felicity gave a laugh that was decidedly false. "This is a brand-new outfit."

"Come on, Felicity. How much damage can one baby do in two minutes?" She and Michael shared a quick, private smile. "I just need to throw on some clothes and run a comb through my hair. Anyway, Timmy likes you."

Felicity acquiesced reluctantly, handling the infant like an unwieldy sack of potatoes.

This time around, Timmy, having lost his fascination with Felicity's necklace and not at all pleased with being passed about, broke into a loud wail. Maddie merely smiled reassuringly and turned to leave the room.

Felicity looked panic-stricken as she called after her daughter. "Maddie. Maddie, wait. You're wrong. I don't think he likes me one bit."

Maddie and Michael both grinned. "Just relax," they said in unison.

Before her mother could argue, Maddie dashed off for the bathroom. Michael called out to her that he'd wait until she came back to say goodbye.

"Why don't you take him, Michael." There was a pleading note in Felicity's voice as Timmy continued to cry.

"Just hoist him over one shoulder and pat his back. That usually settles him down."

Felicity looked doubtful, but she did what Michael suggested. It took a minute to calm Timmy down, but the change of position did the trick. Michael noted that the smile of accomplishment on Felicity's face was remarkably similar to the one he'd seen on Maddie's.

He smiled back at her and found himself beginning to like Felicity Sargent. While Maddie's mother was clearly a charming, vivacious and attractive woman, five minutes with her and he could see why Maddie and Felicity would not have a very close relationship. The woman was more than a little self-involved. Still, as he

watched her soothing Timmy, once again observing
that glimmer of wistfulness in her hazel eyes, he wondered if there wasn't more depth and feeling to Felicity
than either he or Maddie imagined.

When Maddie came back to the living room a few
minutes later, she stood quietly at the entry for a moment, unobserved. Michael and Felicity were sitting
together on the couch chatting softly while Timmy was
stretched out stomach down across Felicity's lap. She
jogged the baby lightly, much to his delight.

"I used to do this with Maddie when she was fussy,"
Felicity was saying. "It was such a long time ago. How
much we forget." And then, rubbing Timmy's back, she
said more to herself than to Michael, "It went by so
quickly. Too quickly."

Maddie was surprised and touched by Felicity's
manner and words. A poignancy washed over her in a
warm tide as she tried to imagine her mother holding,
caressing, soothing her as an infant. She had always
thought her mother couldn't wait for those days to pass,
couldn't wait until her daughter was old enough to ship
off to boarding school. Was it really possible she looked
back on those days with a wistful remembrance?

Michael rose as he spotted Maddie standing silently
in the entry. Their eyes met and held for an instant.
Maddie had the distinct feeling that Michael could read
her thoughts.

He smiled at her, then glanced down at Felicity. "It
was a pleasure meeting you, Mrs. Sargent."

"Felicity, please. Mrs. Sargent sounds so formal. So
old."

"Felicity," Michael repeated warmly. "I'm sure we'll
meet again if you're going to be in Boston for a few days.
I'll be back on Friday."

"I should be in town until the middle of next week. Then I fly to Paris." She rose, having a bit of trouble doing it gracefully as she struggled with the squirming baby. Both Maddie and Michael noted that she made no move to relinquish him, however. "I always stay at the Ritz. Perhaps you and Maddie will stop by and have a drink with me over the weekend."

Michael glanced at Maddie, trying to get a reading. She didn't seem averse to the idea. "Maybe Sunday. My sister is getting married on Saturday."

"Sunday would be fine."

Maddie walked over to her mother. "I'll take Timmy now. See—" her voice caught for a moment "—you did fine."

Felicity seemed pleased by the compliment. She gave Timmy's back an affectionate pat. "If Linda doesn't get back Sunday to retrieve her son, by all means bring Timmy along, darling. But do bring a bottle for him. I doubt the bartender specializes in infant cocktails."

Maddie laughed. "We don't have to worry about it. Linda swore she'd be back on Friday. And if she doesn't show up, I'm going to hop a plane to wherever she is and return her bundle of joy." She grinned at Timmy. "Nothing personal, Scout, but I do have other pressing matters to attend to."

Felicity tilted her head. "Well, I must say, Madeline, you do fit the maternal role far better than I would have imagined."

Maddie felt her cheeks warm, and she deliberately avoided Michael's eye.

Felicity, however, brought him into the conversation by asking his opinion.

Michael gave Maddie a pensive look. "She's quite wonderful at it."

Maddie felt an incredible warmth suffuse her. "So are you," she found herself saying, meeting his gaze at last. Maddie found it difficult to believe, but she spotted a flush rising in Michael's tanned face. She smiled at him, adding to his discomfort.

"I'd better get going," he said, his tone a little stiff.

"I'll walk you to the door." There was a touch of disappointment in her voice.

"Well, give me the child, then, while you say goodbye," Felicity offered.

"That's okay."

But Felicity pried him from her daughter's arms. "Go on."

At the front door Maddie and Michael stood awkwardly. After a few silent moments he leaned down and gave her a peck on the cheek.

"Friday, then?"

Maddie nodded. They both reached for the doorknob at the same time. Maddie drew her hand away, leaving Michael to open the door. He took a step out, stopped, then pivoted slightly.

Maddie smiled, bent on nonchalance. "See you." Damn those mesmerizing eyes of his. How was she supposed to play it cool when those dark eyes radiated such heat?

He touched her hair. Then after a brief hesitation he leaned forward, brushing her lips. That barest kiss made her feel woozy.

Just as she was swaying toward him, Michael impulsively grabbed her wrist, drew her out into the hall, slammed the door shut and kissed her fully, all in the same movement.

He left her leaning against the wall just outside her door, breathless, smiling dizzily. Not wanting to risk testing her balance, she stayed put until he gave her a final wave and stepped into the elevator.

Maddie let out a ragged breath. Then composing herself as best she could, she reached for the doorknob only to realize Michael had locked her out. Embarrassed and still a little flustered, she rang the bell.

"Who is it?" came Felicity's wry voice.

"Very amusing. Open the door, Felicity," Maddie replied sharply, her voice still husky from having been so thoroughly kissed.

Felicity was smiling broadly as she opened the door. Even Timmy wore an impish smile.

Maddie's composure, not completely stable, anyway, completely crumbled. She looked as if she might cry.

"Is being in love really that ghastly?" quipped Felicity.

This time Maddie didn't bother to deny it. She managed a wry smile. "Well, darling," she mimicked her mother, "it does take some preparation. Michael caught me completely unawares."

Felicity grinned. "It's about time. I can tell you now, Maddie, that I've been rather worried about you. It's all well and good to have a flourishing career, but there are no medals to be won for doing it alone."

"You've managed perfectly well alone. And so have I—until Michael arrived. Oh, I know you've had involvements with men, but you've always managed to stay levelheaded. My head has been spinning practically since I laid eyes on Michael."

"You're wrong about me, Maddie. Oh, it's been rare, but there have been one or two men in my life that made me reel. Your father, for one."

"My father?" Maddie looked at her mother curiously. "Really?"

Felicity's expression was a bit sad. "My problem is that I've always been attracted to the wrong men—men who fled responsibility, men who were too attuned to being fancy-free."

"Well, then I've inherited your problem, Felicity," Maddie said wearily. "Michael comes from a huge family. His father died when he was a boy, and he's been saddled with so many responsibilities that the very idea of taking on any new ones scares the living daylights out of him. And to further follow in your shoes, I've gone and allowed myself to fall for a man I very much hope to be working with." She went on to explain about the contract she was angling to get with Barrett's.

"I don't see why it can't work out, Maddie. I adore your line of skin-care products. If Michael needs any further proof, he can have my endorsement. I wouldn't worry about a thing if I were you."

Felicity sounded so optimistic that Maddie's spirits began to lift. Two minutes later they fell swiftly.

Just as she was putting on Timmy's snowsuit to take him with her to the office, the phone rang again.

This time it was Liz on the line, sounding frazzled and upset.

"You'd better get down here on the double, Maddie. A water pipe burst in one of the labs, and it's bedlam around her. I've already put in a half-dozen calls to the building maintenance crew, but it seems we aren't the only ones in the building with the problem. They say they're taking us all in turn. Meanwhile we're wading about in a couple of inches of water. Several experiments got fouled up in the process, and Crawford is having a bird."

"I get the picture," Maddie said wearily. "Just hold the fort. I'll soothe Crawford when I get there. Give me ten minutes."

"More problems?" Felicity asked, observing her daughter's morose expression as she hung up the phone.

"I've got to run. A pipe burst."

"Oh, dear."

Maddie was pulling on her coat. "I'll speak to you later." She threw a scarf around her neck and opened the front door.

Only as she saw her daughter start to leave did Felicity realize Maddie was leaving something—or more precisely some*one*—behind. "Maddie. Wait. Wait a minute. Timmy. You almost forgot Timmy."

Maddie came to an abrupt stop. "Oh..." She scowled. "Well, I can't take him now, Felicity. It's chaos down at the office. You'll just have to cope."

Felicity had difficulty taking in Maddie's words.

"No... you don't mean... cope with Timmy?"

Maddie hurried back and gave her mother a quick hug. "It's a cinch. I even have a supply of disposable diapers in the spare room. They're a breeze. Call me if you have any problems. I'll try to get back early."

"Any problems? Hold on, Maddie. Maddie. Get back here." She watched her daughter race down the hall. "Come back here this instant, Madeline."

Maddie waved without turning, quickly heading for the stairs to be sure her mother didn't corral her before the elevator came.

"Maddie. Please don't do this to me." Felicity watched the service door close and stared wanly down at Timmy. "She's gone."

"ONE CRISIS UNDER CONTROL." Maddie sighed, leaned back in her swivel chair and ran her fingers through her blond hair. When the phone rang, Liz motioned her to stay put and ran out to her office to pick it up, saying she was expecting a call.

Five minutes later Liz reappeared at the door.

"You're not going to like this," she said hesitantly.

"What now?" Maddie looked up from her paper-work. She was hardly in the mood for any further bad news.

"Actually, it's not confirmed."

"Liz."

"That was Colin Akers on the phone. One of our sales reps down in Palm Beach."

"And," Maddie prodded, although for the life of her, she didn't know why. She was sure that whatever Liz had to say was just going to add to her misery. Her only miscalculation was in degree.

"Akers happened to run into a salesman he knows from L'Amour this morning. And this salesman just happened to mention in passing that—" Liz took a deep breath "—Barrett's signed L'Amour for their exclusive skin-care line yesterday. This is all thirdhand, but it seems Harrington pretty much struck the deal with them last Friday."

Maddie couldn't absorb what Liz was saying. Meanwhile Liz was getting more and more fired up.

"The low-down bastard. Oh, I know Harrington told you we had some competition. But what he didn't mention was that he'd already made his choice before he got to Boston on Saturday. What I don't understand is why he didn't tell you Sargent didn't stand a chance. Why string you along?" Liz stopped abruptly, wishing she could swallow her words. "Oh, Maddie, I'm sorry."

A hundred different feelings and responses raced through Maddie's mind, but in the end she just stared at Liz, dazed.

"I can't believe he'd do that to me. Not Michael," she muttered to herself. "Just to get me in bed? He wouldn't. He isn't like that."

"What about that other deal he mentioned to you? Maybe he really does have something better in the works. Or maybe Akers got it wrong." Liz didn't sound convinced or convincing about either possibility.

Maddie never had bought Michael's line about a better deal. What deal could be better than an exclusive skin-care line with Barrett's? And if he thought she could be appeased by some third-rate consolation prize, he had another think coming.

She stared dolefully at Liz. "Maybe you're right. Maybe Akers got it wrong." But she didn't believe it for one instant.

FELICITY CALLED close to noon to check on Maddie's lunch plans.

"Why . . . she left over an hour ago. She said she was going home," Liz said, trying unsuccessfully to hide the worry in her voice.

"It only takes twenty minutes, even in traffic. And there isn't much traffic in the late morning."

"Maybe she stopped off to do some errands."

"Liz, what's wrong? Is Maddie all right? You sound odd."

"Oh . . . it's just that we found out that a deal Maddie was working on fell through."

"What deal?"

Liz clammed up. Maddie might not appreciate her spreading the news.

"Liz."

"I'm sorry, Mrs. Sargent. I'm swamped with work here. I'm sure Maddie will be home soon. She can tell you about it."

"You don't mean the Barrett's deal?" Felicity asked in disbelief.

"Please, Mrs. Sargent. I probably shouldn't have said anything. You know Maddie."

"Maddie's been surprising me lately."

Liz couldn't help smiling, despite her misery. "Me, too."

"Oh, I think I hear the key turning in the lock. That must be her now. Take care, Liz."

Maddie looked calm as she entered her apartment—deadly calm. Her complexion was the color of chalk. Felicity observed her closely, worriedly, but Maddie did not make eye contact.

"How about a cup of tea?" Felicity asked innocuously. Better to take this slow. She had never seen her daughter look more vulnerable. "It's bitter cold out today." She watched Maddie slowly, silently remove her coat, pull off her boots.

"I'll just go put on some water for tea," Felicity said after receiving no response from Maddie.

From the kitchen she called out, "You'll be pleased to know Timmy and I got along famously. You were right. Those disposable diapers are a snap. Oh, I gave him a bottle about an hour ago. He's been taking a nap ever since." She listened but couldn't hear Maddie moving about. After setting the kettle on the stove, she stuck her head out of the kitchen, but the living room was empty.

"Maddie, where are you?" Felicity started down the hall, peeked into the spare room to see Timmy sound asleep, then headed on to Maddie's room. She knocked softly.

When there was no answer, Felicity opened the door gingerly. "Maddie . . ."

Her daughter was sitting on her bed, a bright red dress crumpled in her arms. Head down, Maddie mumbled, "I'd almost forgotten. I've got to go down to the cleaners. They destroyed . . . my dress."

Felicity opened the door wider and crossed the room. She sat down on the bed beside her daughter. Gently she stroked her hair. "Tell me about it, Maddie. Don't hold it in." She could feel her daughter's whole body tense, but her face remained stoically calm.

"There's nothing to talk about, Felicity. It was just a . . . mad day at work."

"I see. Always the brave one, aren't you. So strong, so independent, so self-sufficient. You're going to handle this on your own, is that it?"

Maddie flinched. "I've been doing it all my life, haven't I? Just like you."

"It's been a mistake. For me. And for you. When we hold everything in, we only succeed in tying ourselves in knots. It makes the pain that much worse."

Felicity continued to stroke her daughter's hair, despite Maddie's stiffness.

"I'm all right, Felicity."

"It was the Barrett's account that fell through, wasn't it? And Michael didn't tell you."

Maddie's knuckles whitened as she fiercely gripped the red dress. "I've really got to take this dress to the dry cleaners and demand my money back. They had no right . . ." Her voice caught. "No right." She felt terribly cold. "I trusted him...them. The dry cleaners." Her head was ringing, her throat closing up. She gulped in

some air, trying to fight back the sob she felt forming
in her chest.

Felicity slipped her arm around her daughter's
shoulders. "Poor baby," she whispered. "Poor baby."

Maddie lifted her head, looking at her mother, tears
flooding her eyes, Felicity's face dissolving.

And then, throwing her arms around her mother,
Maddie could hold the floodgates back no longer.
Words spilled out through her sobs. "Oh, Felicity... I
love him so. He lied to me. He deceived me. Oh, it hurts
so much."

Felicity held her daughter tightly in her arms, rock-
ing her, kissing the top of her head.

Maddie clung to her mother as she sobbed.

"I'm glad I'm here, baby." Felicity's voice was hardly
more than a whisper. "I know how much you're hurt-
ing. I do. I truly do. I'll help you, darling. You'll see. It
will be okay. I promise." Felicity felt her own tears
stream down her face, felt the sting of mascara in her
eyes. She paid it no mind. And Maddie, as angry as
she'd always secretly been that her mother had never
before been there for her, took great comfort from her
nearness.

They sat together on the bed, both crying, holding
each other, murmuring words that didn't have to be
clearly heard to be understood. Finally Maddie took her
mother's hand. "Thanks, Mom," she whispered. "This
time it was not a slip of the tongue." There was more
she wanted to say, but the words wouldn't come. And
for the first time Maddie realized they weren't necessary.

11

"COME INTO THE KITCHEN." Felicity took her daughter's arm. "I'll make you a sandwich. You should eat something."

Maddie let her mother lead her from the bedroom, a wispy smile on her tear-streaked face.

Felicity caught the smile and grinned. "I know. I sound just like a mother, don't I?"

Maddie stopped and observed her mother closely. "I like it."

Felicity actually blushed. "Know something? So do I." She sniffed demurely.

Maddie gently rubbed her mother's cheek. "Your mascara ran."

"I must look a sight."

Maddie's hand moved to her own face. "Me, too."

Felicity put her arm around Maddie's shoulder. "Who cares?"

As they passed the spare room, they heard Timmy stirring. Instinctively Maddie turned toward the room. But Felicity stopped her. "You go into the kitchen and heat up a bottle. I'll see to Timmy."

Maddie tilted her head. "Are you sure?"

Felicity gave one of Maddie's ears an affectionate tug. "Some people get into having a second childhood. Why not a second motherhood?"

Maddie shook her head slowly. "You amaze me, Felicity. I never suspected . . ."

Felicity was pensive. "I'm not really sure I did, either." She opened the door to the spare room, pausing for a second to glance over her shoulder at Maddie. "He is a sweet baby."

Maddie nodded. "Yes, he is."

Felicity waved her on. "Don't make the milk too hot, now."

"No. No, I won't."

Five minutes later, while Maddie was pouring the bottle, Felicity entered with a cheerful, newly diapered and dressed baby in her arms.

Maddie screwed on the nipple. "He needs his medicine. When I rushed out this morning, I forgot to tell you."

"Is he ill?" Felicity's voice registered concern. She scrutinized Timmy. "He looks fine."

"Oh, it's just an ear infection."

Felicity pursed her lips. "You had them, too."

"I did?"

"Once the doctor even considered having these tubes inserted in your ears. It sounded so dreadful. I was horrified, even though he said everything he could to try to convince me you wouldn't feel a thing. I remember I was so relieved when he said it wouldn't be necessary after all."

Maddie didn't know what to say. It was astonishing to suddenly see and hear her mother talking and behaving just like . . . a mother.

Felicity handed Timmy over to Maddie for his medicine and then his bottle, and she headed for the refrigerator. "Are you hungry?"

"No, but you must be."

Felicity turned to her daughter. "How about if we share a sandwich. And then...if you like...we can talk about what happened."

Maddie stiffened immediately and was about to protest. She didn't want to talk about what had happened. She didn't want to talk about Michael. She didn't want to think about him. She didn't want to see him ever again.

Felicity turned to the refrigerator and examined the contents. "Now, let's see," she said before Maddie could say anything. "What shall I make?"

"There are some cold cuts in the meat section. And the bread is on top of the fridge."

"Wonderful." Felicity pulled out the bin and removed three deli-wrapped packages. Then she took out mustard and retrieved the loaf of bread.

As Felicity set busily to work, Maddie watched her mother with a mixture of wonder and sadness. She couldn't recall a single instance in her entire childhood that was in any way reminiscent of this scene. She remembered fantasies, sparked by TV shows, of her mother making her her favorite sandwiches, pouring her large glasses of milk, promising cookies if she ate everything on her plate. But for as long as Maddie could recall, it had always been baby-sitters, housekeepers and neighbors who'd actually fixed her lunches. Unless they'd gotten a dinner invitation from a friend or colleague of Felicity's, dinners when she and Felicity were together were always in restaurants. Restaurants were not luxuries with Felicity. They were a tradition.

Felicity generously piled meat on one slice of bread, got Maddie's approval for the mustard and spread it meticulously on another slice of bread, then made up the sandwich and cut it in two.

"Can you manage, holding Timmy?" Felicity asked as she put one part of the sandwich on a plate and carried it over to where Maddie was sitting.

"Nothing to it," Maddie replied. "Since I've had Timmy, I've discovered that mothers, even stand-ins, quickly learn how to be octopuses."

"Yes," Felicity concurred. "A definite requirement. I often wished, when you were a baby, that I had an extra pair of hands." She sat down across the table from Maddie, placing her own half sandwich on the colorful rainbow place mat. But she made no move toward it.

"Go on," Felicity urged. "Take a bite and tell me how it is."

Maddie had to smile. From the look of anxious concern on Felicity's face, her mother might have been asking her to sample a very tricky culinary masterpiece. Cradling Timmy in one arm, Maddie picked up the sandwich and took a bite. "Delicious," she said even before she'd finished chewing.

Felicity smiled, pride glistening in her eyes as she took a bite of her own sandwich. "Well, not quite Rossi's, but not bad."

Timmy gulped down the last of his bottle as Maddie and Felicity finished eating. Felicity rose. "Here, give me Timmy. He needs to be burped." She smiled at her daughter's bemused expression. "I know it probably comes as a surprise, Madeline, but I used to get quite a few hardy burps out of you."

Maddie grinned. "Never."

Felicity lifted Timmy against one shoulder, remembering at the last minute to squeeze a dish towel between Timmy and her shoulder in case he spit up. "It's amazing how it all comes back. Like riding a bike." She paused in the midst of a pat. "Not that I ever did learn how to ride a bike." She went back to rhythmically patting Timmy's back as she leaned against the counter, but her eyes rested a little sadly on her daughter. "I never did learn everything I should have about being a mother." There was regret in her voice. "I sometimes wish I could have been different."

"Different how?" Maddie asked softly.

"We both missed out on so many experiences together. I never went to one of your lacrosse games, and I missed all those school Christmas plays where you flitted about the stage as an angel, and where you once got to be one of the wise men."

Maddie stared at her mother. "I never thought you even knew I'd once been a wise man."

Felicity smiled wistfully. "I did keep track of all your activities. You probably never believed I wanted to be at any of them, but you were wrong. I did. But I couldn't. I suppose I could make a lot of excuses, but I won't. I may have had to have a career because of our circumstances. But I won't say I regretted it. I have always loved what I do. I was good at it from the start. But caring for a baby... I was so overwhelmed about the awesome responsibility of motherhood. You were so little, so helpless. And I was supposed to be strong, confident. I wasn't. I felt scared and helpless, too."

Maddie's eyes blurred with tears. "I was so lonely at all those dreary boarding schools. I felt so abandoned." The words burst forth from her so angrily that they startled her as much as they did Felicity.

Felicity nodded, not trying to defend herself, but refusing to make apologies, either. "I wish I'd been better at juggling a career and motherhood. Single motherhood, I should say. I did do my best. I was often very

lonely, too. There was many a night when I sat in some
silent, far-off hotel room fighting the impulse to simply call your school and demand they put you on the
very next plane. Our times together were all too brief.
But I felt it wasn't fair to disrupt your life. Maybe I was
wrong."

Her mother's words mitigated some of Maddie's suf-
fering. She could finally believe that her mother had
truly cared about her. She had truly loved her. And her
own experience with Timmy and, yes, with Michael
this past week had helped Maddie see how difficult and
painful love and motherhood could be.

Just then Timmy let out a loud, uninhibited burp.
Both women laughed, diffusing the bittersweet mood.

Timmy looked at the two women and giggled.

"He is an adorable baby," Maddie said.

Felicity looked at her daughter with a tender smile.
"Not nearly as adorable as you were." Abruptly she
handed Timmy to her daughter and went out to the hall
to retrieve her purse. She returned to the kitchen and
plucked out her wallet, flipping it open to the picture
section.

There was only one photo amidst the half-dozen
plastic holders. It was old and frayed around the edges.

Felicity very carefully extracted it and handed it to
Maddie.

Maddie stared down at the photo in silence for a long
time as her mother stood behind her.

"See how darling you were," Felicity said softly. "You
so loved to snuggle against me like that. You were just
about Timmy's age when that was snapped. I'd just
taken you from your crib. You were still a little sleepy,
but the moment you saw me smile, you smiled back."
Felicity reached into her purse, pulled out a handker-

chief and swiped at her eyes. "See. You were a beautiful baby, Maddie. A sweet, beautiful, perfect baby." Felicity put her arm around Maddie and drew her back against her heart.

"If I've taught you only one thing, darling," Felicity said soothingly, "it was to go after what you wanted. I never wanted you to deprive yourself of anything. I'm not just talking about having a career, Maddie. I'm talking about love. True love. Enduring love. A love you're willing to fight for. I know Michael's hurt you, but perhaps when he explains . . ."

Maddie shook her head against her mother's breast. "No. I don't want his explanations. I don't want anything from him ever again."

Felicity stroked her daughter's hair. "We'll see," she said softly. "You may change your mind."

"No, I won't," Maddie said adamantly, straightening. She turned around to look up at her mother and grasped her hand. "You've got to help me, Mother. If he comes back on Friday, I can't see him. I can't. You will help me?"

Felicity bent and kissed the top of her daughter's head. "I promise, Maddie. You leave Michael Harrington to me." There was a glint of a mother hen in her hazel eyes. "You may not want to talk to him, my girl, but there are a few words I have to say to the man."

Maddie managed a faint smile. She might have lost a lover this morning, but she'd gained a mother.

MICHAEL LANDED IN BOSTON at five p.m. on Friday. He was feeling terrific. His meetings with Barrett and Epstein had gone better than he'd hoped. There was still a lot of groundwork to be done, but he had set the wheels in motion. And he was confident enough of the plan going through to finally be able to tell Maddie about the offer. That also meant it was time to tell her about L'Amour, but he was sure this new offer would more than make up for any disappointment she'd feel at having lost out to the competition. Now everything Michael wanted for Maddie would work out.

He stepped into a phone booth at the terminal and called his sister Cindy.

"Hi! Listen, I just landed. What time is the rehearsal dinner?"

"Seven o'clock. Why don't you come straight over, have a drink and relax a little before the Mad Hatter tea begins?"

He laughed and glanced at his watch. "Mmm, no, I have a couple of stops to make. I'll be there at six forty-five."

"Are you coming alone?"

"Huh?"

Cindy laughed. "Are you bringing Maddie?"

Michael absently rubbed his jaw. "I . . . don't think so."

"Why don't we leave it open? We can always squeeze one more at the table. See how she feels about it when you stop over there now."

Michael laughed. "You don't miss a thing, do you, Cin?"

"I'd like to think I was a wiz at ESP, but the truth is, bro, you are about as transparent as a piece of plate glass."

"Don't get carried away, Cindy. Maddie's a terrific woman. And we do have . . . certain feelings for each other. But—"

"Skip the speech, Michael. You'll only be wasting your breath on my account. You can't convince me you're not hooked. And if you really think you can talk yourself out of your feelings, well, do it on your own time. I, for one, hope you fail. I like her. Tell her so when you see her."

Flustered, Michael muttered, "Yeah, right. I'll see you later."

After he hung up the phone, he stared at it for a minute. Should he call Maddie from here and tell her he planned to stop by for a few minutes before the rehearsal dinner? He'd hoped to get back to Boston earlier in the day, but it hadn't worked out. After checking his watch again, he decided she was probably en route home. Best to head straight for her apartment.

Getting out of the parking lot at the airport at rush hour was no easy matter. It took a certain amount of aggressiveness and cleverness, both of which, fortunately, Michael Harrington had plenty of.

Within five minutes he was heading down the expressway. He yawned suddenly. It had been a hectic three days. And, he admitted, part of his exhaustion had come from expending so much energy fending off enticing visions of Maddie. They sprang up at random, catching him unawares. At his apartment. At meetings with Barrett and Epstein. At restaurants. Waiting for cabs.

Maddie. He could see her so clearly. Laughing. Blushing. Holding Timmy soothingly in her arms. Lying naked on her bed, her fine, beautiful body glowing with warmth, passion. That body that was so perfectly in tune with his. Maddie.

He was stalled in traffic for over a half hour before finally making it through the Callahan Tunnel, but once he got on the Southeast Expressway, he adeptly weaved in and out of the traffic onto Storrow Drive and got to Maddie's place by six.

Damn, he thought, racing through the lobby, impatiently pressing the button for the elevator. He wasn't going to have much time with Maddie. And no time to shower or change before the dinner.

The elevator creaked to Maddie's floor. He hurried down the hall to her apartment, wondering if Timmy would still be there or if Linda had already come for him. He actually missed the tyke.

He rang the doorbell. What was taking her so long? Maybe she wasn't home yet. He pressed the bell again.

"Yes, who is it?"

A woman's voice, but not Maddie's. Felicity. Yes, that was who it was.

"It's me, Felicity. Michael Harrington."

"Oh."

Michael was puzzled by her tone, even more puzzled by how long it took Felicity to unlock and open the door. And then it was only a third of the way.

"Isn't Maddie home yet?" He gave Felicity a curious look. Where was all that charm and vivaciousness? Her face was as stoic and rigid as if it had been carved in granite.

"Maddie is home." Her voice was as cold as ice—like an icicle piercing Michael's buoyant feelings, collapsing them.

"What's wrong?"

"Maddie does not want to see you."

"What does that mean?"

"Really, Mr. Harrington, I believe you know perfectly well what that means."

"Okay, then why doesn't she want to see me?"

"I believe, Mr. Harrington, you know the answer to that question, as well."

Michael's dark eyes narrowed. "I don't know what's going on, Felicity—"

"Mrs. Sargent," she corrected archly.

"This is crazy. I want to see Maddie. Whatever's going on, I'd like to hear it from her."

"No, Mr. Harrington. You'll hear it from me. And you'll hear it in spades. You pulled a lousy trick on my daughter. You lied to her, deceived her and manipulated your way into her bed. That's bad enough, Mr. Harrington. But you also manipulated your way into her heart. And Maddie's heart happens to be very precious to me. You've broken it. She's in love with you. Not that that means much to someone like you. You, Mr. Harrington, define love as L'Amour, don't you? L'Amour. Personally—" she thrust back her shoulders "—I think they're a second-rate skin-care company." She started to slam the door, but Michael's hand shot out.

"Look, I can explain."

"I couldn't care less about your explanations."

Rage threatened to overtake him. He fought for control, nevertheless pushing at the door. "I want to explain to Maddie."

"You're no doubt stronger than I am, Mr. Harrington, and you can no doubt push your way in here. But I assure you, Maddie will not talk to you. And if you persist, I shall call the police and inform them that we have an intruder."

Michael stared at her, his hand still pressed against the door but no longer pushing on it. "I didn't mean to hurt her. Damn it, it's the last thing I wanted. Don't you know that?"

"I know that Maddie must have seen something special in you that she's never seen in another man." Felicity's voice softened a fraction. "That's the real tragedy of it. If the only crime you'd committed was in the name of business, Maddie would have been angry and hurt, but those wounds would have healed. In many ways, she's tough and determined. She'll find other deals, perhaps better ones. But the wounds you've inflicted go deeper, Mr. Harrington."

He leaned wearily against the doorjamb, his hand still on the door to prevent it being slammed in his face. "I need to talk to her, Feli—Mrs. Sargent. Okay, I should have told her about L'Amour straightaway. But . . . it just got so complicated. I wasn't trying to manipulate her. God, I was as far from being in control of a situation as I've ever been. It all happened so fast. I never dreamed . . ." He saw that Felicity wasn't really listening, that she'd already made up her mind, tried him and found him guilty. And from her perspective, why not? He was guilty.

It was getting late. Even if he did force his way in and get to Maddie, there wouldn't be time to explain, to sort it out with her.

A little vein pulsed in his temple. He took a deep breath. "Whether or not you believe it, Mrs. Sargent, I'm on Maddie's side. I told her I was working on a new angle for her. Well, it's really looking good. If I could just see her . . ."

Felicity remained stoic.

Michael swallowed his frustration. "Okay, Mrs. Sargent, you win this round. But the fight isn't over. Not by a long shot."

After Felicity closed the front door, Maddie stepped out of her room holding Timmy.

Felicity turned to her. "He'll be back."

Maddie shrugged.

"He wants to explain. He says he has a new deal for you."

Maddie laughed derisively.

"There is a chance you might be wrong about the man."

"I wish I'd never met him. I hate feeling like such a little fool."

Felicity walked over to her daughter. She could see circles under Maddie's eyes. "There's absolutely nothing foolish about being in love."

"Who said anything about love?" Maddie retorted too quickly.

"Maybe you should talk to him, Maddie."

"No."

Timmy began to fuss in Maddie's arms, and Felicity took him. "What time did Linda say she'd be here? She phoned almost an hour ago."

"By seven." Maddie stared at Timmy, an enigmatic expression on her face. "If it weren't for Timmy..." Maddie stopped, fighting back tears.

Felicity put her free arm around Maddie and held her close. "Come on. We'll bathe, feed and change Timmy so that Linda can take him straight home and tuck him into bed."

Maddie smiled faintly as she stepped back. "I do think you've grown quite fond of that baby, Mother."

Felicity smiled back. "I do believe you're right." There were tears in her eyes. "If you ever do marry and have children, Maddie, I rather think I'd make a more than satisfactory grandmother." She took her daughter's hand. "And you, darling, would make a wonderful mother."

"Don't. Please." There was helplessness and pleading in Maddie's voice.

"Talk to him, Maddie."

"I can't. I can't risk any more hurt."

"That's not the only possible outcome."

"Yes, it is," Maddie said so sharply that Timmy started to fuss. But Felicity had him under control very quickly. "Don't you see?" Maddie went on, following her mother to the kitchen. "It isn't just that he lied about the L'Amour deal. Michael's made it perfectly clear from the start that he wasn't looking for anything lasting. No promises. No marriage. No strings."

"Oh, darling, they all say that at first."

"Michael means it. He's dead set against getting married and having kids."

Felicity ordered Maddie to run a bath for Timmy in the sink as she undressed him. "Last I remember, darling," she said casually, slipping the baby's terry suit off, "you felt exactly the same way. You have always been determined to take the world on by yourself."

Maddie dangled her fingers in the warm running water. *I don't need him. I'll stop feeling wretched without him.* It had happened so fast. That was the problem. One minute she had Michael, great plans for her company, laughter, passion, joy. The next minute everything had changed. Michael was gone, prospects were gone. A pain twisted through her middle . . . like a labor pain, she suddenly imagined.   •

She turned and stared wanly at her mother. In a voice that came out strangled, she whispered, "I'm tired of taking the whole world on alone."

"Maddie . . ."

"Let's drop the subject, Felicity."

Felicity smiled knowingly. Maddie hadn't called her by her first name in days. Her use of it now was a clear indication that she desperately needed a little breathing room. Felicity understood.

"Here we go," she said, handing Timmy to Maddie. "You bathe him and I'll fix him some baby cereal."

Maddie gave her mother an appreciative nod and set to the task, thinking, as Timmy slapped merrily at the water, that she was going to miss him, too.

When Linda arrived arm in arm with her husband, Donald, a little past seven to retrieve Timmy, both Felicity and Maddie relinquished him reluctantly. But they were thrilled that Donald was the one to gather Timmy in his arms and give his son a warm, affectionate kiss. Linda hugged Maddie, thanking her profusely for giving her and Donald a chance to get everything straightened out.

After beaming parents and son departed, the apartment felt sadly empty and disturbingly quiet. Maddie turned on the radio, but the soft rock music only served to heighten the loss.

Felicity watched Maddie pretend to read a magazine as she sat across from her in the living room. Finally Maddie threw the magazine down on the coffee table and folded her arms across her chest. Felicity rose, walked silently over to the couch and sat down at the opposite end, patting her lap. "You look exhausted, baby. Come, stretch out. Rest your head on me."

Maddie hesitated for a moment and then did as her mother suggested. Gently Felicity stroked her daughter's brow and smoothed the hair from her face.

Maddie sighed, her body relaxing even if her mind wouldn't. "Mother?"

"Yes."

"Did you ever sing lullabies to me when I was a baby?"

Felicity didn't answer immediately. "No," she said finally. "But I wish I had."

Maddie nodded and closed her eyes. Before she drifted off to sleep, she turned and looked up at her mother. "I love you," she said in a voice that was barely more than a whisper.

MICHAEL WENT THROUGH the motions of host and "father" of the bride like a robot that night. He barely touched his dinner and kept missing cues during the rehearsal. The whole family knew something was amiss. And that something spelled Maddie. But Michael looked daggers at anyone who so much as mentioned her name.

All that evening Felicity's words echoed in his mind. He couldn't shake them off any more than he could shake off visions of Maddie. Only now he saw her white with rage, then stretched across her bed crying, then staring at him, her beautiful hazel eyes filled with fury and pain. Those visions stabbed through him.

There had to be time to straighten things out, he thought. Race back there tonight, after the rehearsal was over, bang on her door, demand to see her. Take her in his arms. Feel her body respond.

Felicity had said she loved him. Was that her interpretation? Or had Maddie told her that she loved him? She'd never told him. He felt cheated.

"Michael, you keep missing the beat. Slow down. You're walking me to the altar, not rescuing me from a burning building," complained his sister Jessie.

"Sorry," he mumbled.

He tried to concentrate, but his mind seemed determined to rebel. *Do I love Maddie? Is that it? I know I want her. I know I can't push her out of my head. I know I feel so damn good with her that I want to sing. I know when I'm making love to her I feel this exhilarating sense of connection. Is that love?*

He broke out in a sweat. He was trembling.

"Come on, Michael. We're almost there," his sister whispered. "Keep the beat and we'll be home free."

Keep the beat. His heart was beating wildly. *Keep the beat. The beat of my heart.*

12

WHEN FELICITY INSISTED on staying with Maddie on Friday night instead of returning to her suite at the Ritz, Maddie didn't argue. She didn't want to be alone. More than that, her mother's presence was proving to be a great comfort.

The next morning, when Maddie awoke a little after ten, Felicity was already in the kitchen.

"Coffee?"

Maddie nodded groggily. She sat down at the kitchen table. Felicity brought over a steaming hot mug.

"It isn't instant," Maddie marveled after taking a sip.

"I detest instant coffee," Felicity said lightly.

Maddie laughed. "I'm just surprised you know how to make fresh coffee."

"I know." Felicity grinned. "You no doubt think all I'm capable of making are reservations. Or dialing room service."

"Well . . ."

"You're right. But if one puts one's mind to coping with a new situation, one can surprise oneself."

Maddie eyed her mother shrewdly. "Somehow I think we've moved from making fresh coffee to making generalizations, Mother."

"Don't you have a wedding to attend this afternoon?"

"I told you last night that, under the circumstances, I'm not going." She glanced at the kitchen clock. "I should call Mrs. Harrington and tell her. I'll wait a little longer."

Felicity studied her daughter carefully. "You look dreadful, darling."

Maddie laughed dryly. "All the more reason not to go to a wedding."

"You aren't going to feel or look better until you confront this matter."

Maddie's eyes narrowed. "Let's not overdo the motherly advice. Really, I'm a big girl now." Immediately after the words were out, Maddie regretted them. She reached out and touched her mother. "I'm sorry. That was nasty."

Felicity gave Maddie a pensive look. "I suppose I am pushing it a bit. It's funny. All these years that you've been grown up I've never really thought you were ever in need of motherly advice. The truth of it is, I've always felt rather in awe of you."

Maddie stared at her mother, wide-eyed. "In awe of me? For heaven's sake, why?"

"Oh, you always seemed so self-contained, so sure of yourself . . . so in control of everything. You never seemed to need anything . . . or anyone."

"But . . . that's exactly how I've always seen you. I was simply following your lead. Never all that successfully."

"You put on a good act."

Maddie observed her mother for several moments. "You put on a better one. I kept wishing I'd be as good at it someday as you."

Felicity shook her head sadly. "It isn't a goal to aspire to, darling, believe me. Oh, it's one thing to have confidence in yourself, to go after your dreams, to feel good about your abilities. But we all need someone. It's only that some of us are more lucky than others at finding that someone."

Maddie stared miserably at her mother. "Yes, some of us are very unlucky." And then, with a whisper of a smile, she added, "At least we've found each other."

Felicity smiled, squeezing her daughter's hand. Then she glanced idly around the room. "I wonder how Timmy is doing back home."

"I know," Maddie said with a sigh. "The apartment doesn't feel the same without him." She sipped her coffee for a bit and then rose. "Well, I'll go take a shower and get dressed." She hesitated. "Then I'll phone Mrs. Harrington."

It was nearly eleven when the doorbell rang. Maddie was in her room dressing. Felicity, still in her robe, went to answer the door.

Who is it?"

"Michael. I'm not leaving until I see Maddie, Mrs. Sargent. You can call the police. Hell, you can call the militia. I have to see her."

Felicity sighed and opened the door. "Oh..." she murmured as she saw him standing there dressed to the nines. Some men looked especially good in tuxedos. Michael Harrington put them to shame. He looked absolutely glorious.

His midnight-blue eyes glinted as he stared Felicity down. "In case Maddie forgot to mention it to you, we have a wedding to attend this afternoon. I've come to pick her up." He brushed past her.

"Wait, Michael. Go into the kitchen and have a cup of coffee. Let me have a word with Maddie."

Michael rubbed his jaw. "This whole thing is driving me crazy. Maddie drives me crazy. I can't sleep. I have no appetite. I can't think straight anymore." He paused. "Okay, I'll go get some coffee."

As Michael headed for the kitchen, Felicity proceeded to Maddie's room with determination in her step.

"Who was at the door?" Maddie asked, slipping a sweater over her head.

Instead of answering, Felicity gave her daughter a tip-to-toe inspection. "Really, darling, that won't do at all."

Maddie looked down at her feet, which were covered by wool socks, her dungarees, her favorite gray mohair sweater. "Won't do for what?"

"For a wedding, of course."

Maddie stepped back, tripped over her shoe and landed on the bed.

"Michael was at the door."

Maddie's heart started to pound. "You *did* send him away. Tell me you sent him away."

Felicity smiled airily. "He's in the kitchen having a cup of coffee."

Maddie was horrified. "In the kitchen? In *my* kitchen? Drinking coffee?"

"My fresh brewed coffee. Oh, dear, it's probably stale by now."

"What is the matter with you, Mother? How can you be thinking about stale coffee at a time like this?"

Felicity shrugged. "Really, dear, I'm not thinking about coffee nearly as much as I'm thinking about what you're going to wear to Michael's sister's wedding." She smiled brightly. "The man looks positively smashing in a tux, Maddie. You'll have to come up with an outfit equally wonderful."

Maddie fought back tears. "Why are you doing this? You said you would help me."

Felicity smiled tenderly. "I'm trying my very best, baby. He loves you, Maddie."

"He told you that?" Maddie stared at her mother in disbelief.

"Well . . . not in so many words."

"Oh, Mother, don't do this to me."

"He's got all the symptoms, darling."

"Oh, no, now you sound like Liz. Symptoms! I'll tell you what you can both do with your symptoms!"

"That's better," Felicity said, unperturbed. "Be angry. It's far more becoming than being miserable. There. There's some color in your cheeks." She walked to the closet. "Now what were you planning to wear to the wedding?"

"I am not going to the wedding."

"I'm afraid Michael is bound and determined to take you. I wouldn't put it past him to cart you off dressed just the way you are now. Wouldn't that be rather embarrassing for you?"

"He wouldn't."

"Shall we find out?"

Maddie was silent.

"Ah, here's a lovely red dress. Oh, no, that's the one you need to take back to the cleaners. Dear, dear. It really did shrink, didn't it?"

Maddie rose reluctantly and stood, arms akimbo. "All right, if it will make you happy, I'll put something appropriate on and go to the wedding. But only because I believe you would actually encourage Michael to drag me off like this. Why you've suddenly taken his side, I don't know. Michael Harrington is not in love with me. He's never said a single word about love. He's never given me one hint of wanting anything more than a casual affair."

She strode over to the closet and pulled out a pretty green chiffon dress. "I'll tell you why I'm really going to the wedding. To prove to you, to Michael, to myself, that I can get along without him just fine."

"Yes, dear."

"I mean it."

Felicity smiled. "Do you need any help?"

Maddie glared at her. "Oh, you've done enough already."

"Well, then, I'll leave you to it." She started for the door. "I'll keep Michael company."

"You do that."

Felicity turned the knob. "I've got a lovely gold pin with me in my pocketbook that would look wonderful on that dress."

"I don't want to look wonderful," Maddie said pointedly.

Fired up the way she was, she couldn't look anything but, Felicity thought.

Maddie stayed in her room for several minutes after she was dressed and ready. The problem was, she wasn't ready. She wasn't ready to face Michael. She'd hoped to have more time, more distance. More fortitude.

She silently rehearsed what she would say, what he would say, what she would answer. The rehearsal only added to her agitation. Her palms were sweaty as she opened the bedroom door. Her legs were shaky as she walked down the hall.

Michael must have heard her. He stepped out of the kitchen into the hall.

The sight of him took Maddie's breath away. The contrast between his tanned, hard-edged features and the refined, well-tailored black tux was devastating. The aura of raw masculinity he exuded was so strong that Maddie had to dig her fingernails into the palm of her hand for control.

The space between them, no more than ten feet, crackled with electricity. Michael's dark eyes drifted from her face, took in her soft green chiffon dress, stunning in its simplicity. He returned his gaze to her face. He could see the heightened color in her cheeks. She was very beautiful. Even at this distance he could detect the faint, inviting scent of her floral perfume. It instantly evoked erotic fantasies, much to his dismay.

"Nice day for a wedding," Maddie said, injecting a note of false brightness into her voice that fooled neither one of them.

Suddenly she realized she was frozen to the spot, in a panic about getting another step closer to him. She felt light-headed, as if she might faint.

Felicity popped her head out of the kitchen and smiled at Maddie. "What a beautiful dress, Maddie. You look wonderful. Doesn't she, Michael?"

Michael was as rooted to his spot as Maddie was to hers. He felt equally light-headed. "Wonderful," he murmured.

"Well, you two had better head off. You know that old song, 'Get Me to the Church on Time.'"

Maddie testing herself, took one step, then another. Okay. She was doing okay.

Michael smiled at her concentration. He began to feel a bit more relaxed. He stepped toward her. Pretty steady. Yeah, he'd be okay.

They were two feet apart. Felicity discreetly slipped back into the kitchen and began banging pots and pans.

Maddie smiled at her mother's obviousness, but without realizing it that smile also took in Michael.

He found her smile dazzling. "You really do look wonderful, Maddie."

Her smile deepened. "Thanks. So do you."

He hesitated. "Listen, Maddie..."

"No, Michael. Not now. Let's just go to the wedding and..." She started to say, "Get through it," but realized that would sound awful.

Michael smiled, and Maddie knew he'd most likely read her thoughts. Oh, well, he had to realize this was going to be an ordeal for her.

An hour later Maddie was distraught to discover that the wedding was proving more of an ordeal than she had expected. As she watched Michael, who was giving the bride away, walking down the aisle with his sister Jessica, Maddie found herself having to fight a crazy sensation that it was her wedding day, not Jessica's. Even her eyes played tricks on her. She could see herself in Jessica's wedding dress, arm in arm with Michael. Only he wasn't giving the bride away. He was marrying her.

The scent of all the flowers decorating the chapel, and the bouquets carried by the bride, flower girl and bridesmaids, had a dizzying effect on Maddie. She fixed her gaze on Michael as he drew nearer her pew. He looked so proud, so regal, so intoxicatingly handsome. He made a perfect...groom.

Michael as groom. She shook herself. Was she truly insane? Insanity continued as her eyes locked for a moment with Michael's. He smiled, and Maddie could have sworn his lips had moved, that he had whispered something to her. It looked like..."I do." Her heart hammered. Her throat was dry. She gripped the pew with whitened knuckles.

The bride swished by in her full-length satin-and-lace Empire gown. Then the flower girl and the brides- maids. They all carried gardenias. Maddie's head whirled. The scent, this close, was cloying. Her vision was blurred.

The setting was too perfect, the fantasy too real. The sight of Michael, in his tuxedo, walking up to the altar, was creating havoc within her.

As she listened to the ceremony, she had to fight back the impulse to cry. People always cried at weddings, but Maddie was afraid that if she started she might not stop.

Michael was standing off to the side of the bride and groom. Maddie tried to avoid looking at him, but her eyes seemed to have a will of their own. His gaze was focused on his sister and the groom. He looked very solemn.

The minister's voice droned on. Michael was only half paying attention. While he trained his eyes on Jes- sie and his soon-to-be brother-in-law, his thoughts were far removed from them. He couldn't fathom the tur- moil inside him. It had been building all morning, but it had begun in earnest when he caught Maddie's eye as he was walking down the aisle with Jessica. The crazy thing was, when he looked from Maddie to his sister, suddenly beneath the bride's net veil, smiling warmly, tenderly, erotically at him . . . was Maddie's face. He'd had to blink several times to dispel the vision. He'd al- most missed a step.

Hazily both Michael and Maddie heard the minister pronounce the happy couple husband and wife. Tears filled Maddie's eyes as they kissed. Michael had to squint to keep the tears from rising in his eyes.

And then, as the couple turned up the aisle, Michael's eye once again caught Maddie's. Her breath caught in her throat.

Oh, Michael, I wish this were our wedding. I wish that it were us walking up the aisle, hand in hand, looking radiant as brides and grooms always do on their wedding day. Oh, Michael...

Mustering all her strength, she pasted on a congratulatory smile, praying that for once Michael would not be able to read her mind.

His own smile was enigmatic. What was he thinking? she wondered. What was he feeling?

After the ceremony Maddie stood on the sidelines as family pictures were taken. At one point Mrs. Harrington pulled her into one of the group shots, insisting that Michael, whom she pushed beside her, put his arm around her. And smile.

The reception was in the church basement. The hundred or more guests feasted from a buffet table, took time out for hugs, kisses and congratulations to the bride, groom and family of each. Before the three-piece band began the dance music, Jessica called all the single women in the room to gather behind her for the throwing of the bouquet.

Maddie ducked behind a group of middle-aged men and women. No way was she going to join in that quaint ritual.

Unfortunately Mrs. Harrington spotted her and motioned vigorously for her to join in. There was no way out of it. Maddie flushed scarlet as Michael caught sight of her trying to make herself scarce in the back of the group. She glared at him as he cocked his head in amusement.

Maddie resolutely kept her hands at her sides as Jessica gave everyone in the group a bright smile and then turned her back to them and tossed.

Maddie stared with complete dismay at the bouquet, which was zeroing in on her. Thank heavens for the aggressive and perhaps desperate young woman on her right. Just in the nick of time, the woman's hand darted out and grabbed the bouquet, accidentally knocking Maddie to the side.

The young woman gave Maddie an apologetic smile. "Oh, I'm sorry. I didn't mean to shove. It's just that this is the fifth wedding I've attended this year. And, well . . . I'd really like the sixth to be mine."

Maddie smiled. "I wish you the best of luck."

A minute later Michael was behind her.

"That was a close call."

"I do believe your sister must have eyes in the back of her head," Maddie said, trying to look amused.

He gave her a considered look. "You certainly were determined not to catch it. Are you superstitious?"

Maddie tried her best to play this coolly. "No. I just didn't want to ruin it for someone who really wanted it."

"I see."

He leaned toward her. For one panicked instant Maddie thought he was going to kiss her. What would happen then to her cool control? It would vanish instantly, that's what.

He didn't kiss her. Instead, he merely asked her to dance. He was smiling, but there was a smoldering look in his eyes.

He put his arm around her waist. He felt her stiffen. "It's only a dance, Maddie."

She wanted to refuse. She wasn't at all sure she could handle even a dance with Michael. To feel his arms around her, his warm breath ruffling her hair, to feel his long, muscular, oh-so-familiar body pressed against hers . . . it was too much. But as she started to turn him down, she saw the implacable set of his jaw, the glint of determination in his eyes.

"All right. One dance. And then I'm leaving."

He pulled her close as the band played an old sentimental fox-trot. "We've never danced together."

She swallowed. No, they'd certainly skipped the usual preliminaries. No wining, dining, dancing, courting. They'd desired each other too much. They hadn't wanted to waste time, play games. And even now Maddie felt that same hungry yearning. Even as her mind rebelled.

Had it been as wonderful for him? Had he felt her tenderness as she had felt his? Would it be as hard for him to forget her as it was going to be for her to forget him?

Maddie broke away as soon as the dance was over. "I have to go."

"I'll drive you."

"No. No, you shouldn't leave."

"I'll come back. The family will understand."

"No. I'd rather get a cab."

"How about dinner tomorrow night?"

Maddie shook her head.

He gripped her wrist and led her off to a quiet corner.

"I know I should have told you about the L'Amour deal straightaway," he started to explain.

"Don't, Michael. That's the way it goes in business. I guess I was naive enough to think . . ." She stopped.

"Well, this experience has helped me to grow up. I'm a big girl now, Michael. Sargent Skin Care will survive without Barrett's. When the next deal comes along, I'll be a lot shrewder, I assure you."

"I've been trying to talk to you about the next deal, damn it, but you won't give me a chance to get a word in. And I really don't want to get into it here. Let's get together tomorrow. Look, I'm not as big a bastard as you are casting me. Give me a chance, Maddie."

"Michael, we had a brief fling. And you can go off knowing you taught me more about passion and business than . . ." She pressed her lips together, trying to steady her breath. "More than I wanted to learn." With that she broke free of his grasp and darted through the merry crowd of celebrants.

MICHAEL HAD TO FLY back to New York on Monday. He called Maddie at work and at home every day that week, but all he got was a secretary or an answering machine. He left messages, insisting that she give him a chance to outline a promising new deal for her. He left his office and home numbers, but Maddie didn't call back.

Maddie, determined not to take any crumbs Michael wanted to throw her way, stubbornly ignored his messages.

On Friday, a clear, crisp day, Maddie decided to take a walk during her lunch break. She strolled down Newberry Street, a quaint Boston thoroughfare lined with little gift shops, art galleries and boutiques. Maddie glanced idly at the window displays, uninterested in doing any shopping until she came to a small toy store. She stared at the displays of dolls, trucks, stuffed animals and, on impulse, walked in and purchased a large white cuddly teddy bear.

She left work early that day, ringing Linda up to say she'd like to stop by and visit her and Timmy. Linda was delighted. Once again she told Maddie she'd be forever grateful to her for helping her get her marriage back together.

Maddie arrived at Linda's doorstep just after four. She felt a little silly holding the giant teddy bear, but she knew Timmy would love it.

"Hi," Linda greeted her cheerily and grinned at the sight of the stuffed animal. "This must be Tim's lucky day. Two visitors bearing gifts. And it isn't even Christmas."

"Two...?" Maddie didn't finish her question. As she stepped in the door, she saw Michael Harrington sitting in the living room merrily bouncing Timmy on his knee.

Maddie's first instinct was to bolt. But Michael had already looked up and so had Timmy. At the sight of her Timmy giggled gleefully. Michael's response was less expressive, but his smile, a little awkward, and charmingly boyish, had a devastating effect on Maddie.

She stood there, unable to look into his eyes. Linda stood behind her.

"Go on in. Michael's been singing your praises again. He keeps telling me how great you were with Timmy. Not that I had any doubt you would be."

"Again?" Maddie echoed, her gaze finally directed at Michael. "You've been here before?"

Michael stood with Timmy in his arms. "I stopped by one other time I was in town for the day. Just to see how he was doing. If he got over his ear infection." He smiled crookedly, redness sneaking up over his collar. "I guess I got kind of attached to him."

Maddie nodded. She didn't know what to say. Michael walked over to her with Timmy. "Why don't you hold him? Or are you nervous again now that you're out of practice?"

Maddie laughed softly. "No. I'm sure it's like riding a bike." She showed Timmy his gift. He grabbed for the bear, and then Maddie took them both in her arms. She walked over to the couch, spotting, as she sat down with Tim, another teddy bear that bore a remarkable resemblance to the one she'd just given the baby.

Michael grinned, dropping into the chair across from her. "I guess we have very similar taste."

Linda stood in the entry. "Hey, you two, can I ask a big favor? I just need to run down to the store for some milk. I'll be back in five minutes. Could you keep an eye on Tim for me?" Michael, ignoring the look of discomfort on Maddie's face, said, "Sure, we'd love to."

Once Linda left, Maddie began busily playing with Timmy.

"You never answered any of my calls, Maddie."

She gave Michael the briefest glance. "I thought you'd get the hint. I don't want to do business with you, Michael." She hesitated, and when she spoke again, she kept her eyes on Timmy. "Or anything else. We had our little fling. No strings, no promises, remember? Well . . . it's over."

"It isn't over, Maddie." He walked over to her, took Timmy in his arms and leveled his gaze on her.

For all her anger and hurt, she couldn't help the flash of arousal that shot through her.

"Linda will be right back, Michael. This isn't the time or the place."

"Okay, then let's go over to your apartment when Linda gets back." It was a statement not a question.

Maddie met his gaze. Only now did she see that his features looked a bit ragged. So this last week hadn't been a breeze for him, either, she thought.

"All right," she relented. "We'll talk back at my place."

13

MICHAEL, USUALLY SO SMOOTH when it came to business—and it was business first, he'd firmly decided—could find no easy way to begin as he stood facing Maddie in her living room. So he dug his hand into his pants pocket and pulled out the tube of the Sargent "wonder cream," tossing it on the coffee table.

Maddie stared at it and then looked up at Michael, puzzled.

"Have you ever heard of Childcare? They're the leading manufacturer of infant furnishings in the country. Last year they broke into infant's clothes. They're already in the black. Barrett's carries their full line."

Michael stopped to take a breath and then sat down in an armchair. Maddie, following his lead, sat across from him on the couch.

He leaned forward. "They've decided to break into a new market. Skin care for babies. Hypoallergenic powders, soaps, shampoos, lotions." His face broke into a smile. "An ointment that really works on diaper rash."

Maddie stared at Michael, but she didn't say a word.

"The president of Childcare is Joel Epstein. A terrific guy. He reviewed your portfolio, had his lab have a go at your wonder cream." He hesitated, then rose, crossed over to the couch and sat down. His eyes burned into her. "He wants you, Maddie."

She kept staring at him.

"No punches pulled. No other companies considered. He's ready to work out a deal with you." He smiled crookedly. "Of course, Barrett's would like the opportunity to introduce the new line. But after the products are introduced into the market, Epstein plans a major marketing campaign and full saturation. Supermarkets, drugstores, department stores. Upscale, downscale. In short, he wants to see Sargent Babycare products in the hands of every concerned mother across the country."

Maddie finally found her voice. "I can't believe it. I never really... considered that market."

"Epstein is willing to invest enough money to enable you to branch out. What do you think?"

Maddie's eyes were wide. "What do I think? It's... fantastic. It's... wonderful."

"It will put Sargent on the map, Maddie. It's what you wanted. What you always dreamed of."

She shifted her weight on the couch. Yes, it was what she wanted. What she'd dreamed of. It was the financial coup of a lifetime. So why did she have this funny, let-down feeling?

"This was what you had in mind for me all along?"

"Well...almost all along," he admitted. "I was wrong to hedge my bet, Maddie. I should have told you about L'Amour straight off. But you'd had quite a night and... I didn't have the heart to tell you. And afterward...I was sure you'd toss me out on my ear. I didn't want you to toss me out, Maddie."

"Is that why you thought up the Childcare deal?"

"I guess there was some of that. And part of it was that I did feel I owed you. But the main reason, Maddie, is that I happen to believe in what you have to offer." He guided her chin in his direction. "If Timmy could talk, he'd say the same."

She smiled. "I don't know what to say. You certainly keep on turning my world topsy-turvy."

"Does that mean you forgive me?"

Her eyes held his steadily. "As long as you promise to play it straight with me from here on out."

Michael grinned. "Scout's honor."

After a few moments he rose from the couch and looked down at her. "Now that we've settled that, we can put business aside." As Maddie's breath caught, he pulled her up to him, his mouth on hers before she could protest. He kissed her roughly, his tongue thrusting past her teeth.

His mouth never left hers as he unzipped her dress. Maddie was conscious of nothing but his lips, his tongue, his hands on her skin, the smell of wool and after-shave lotion.

Only when he began to slip her dress off did Maddie pull back. "I don't think this is wise, Michael."

"It's the smartest thing I've done in two weeks," he murmured into her hair.

Maddie's hazel eyes glistened with excitement. "Maybe you're right."

With a wriggle she was out of the dress. In one swift movement Michael pulled off his sweater. She was unbuttoning his shirt as he lifted her in his arms and carried her into the bedroom.

They finished undressing each other before they fell into bed. Michael stroked her body with possessive tenderness. He whispered wonderful things as he caressed her. He told her how much he missed her, how beautiful she was, how good she felt, how in sync they were. He said every wonderful thing in the world except that he loved her and wanted to marry her, have babies with her, grow old with her. That wasn't part of the deal.

He slid on top of her, and she felt him inside her. Even as she let him draw her into that warm, soft, erotic depth, some part of her felt incomplete. Maddie wasn't sure if Michael sensed the change, but his movements slowed, and with sensitive patience he held back until finally all thought eluded her and she arched against him in ecstasy.

In the pearly grayness of dusk they lay in each other's arms. He stroked her back, kissed her damp hair, rested his free hand between the satiny warmth of her thighs. "Let's stay like this all weekend."

Maddie didn't argue as she snuggled against him. "Mmm, I could stay like this forever."

Michael cupped her chin, his eyes sparkling, his smile tender. "That's not a bad idea, Maddie."

She smiled hesitantly. "Are you serious?"

"You changed my life, Maddie. You and Timmy both. I know we have this...no-strings deal and all. But what if I wanted to renegotiate? Make a new deal with you?"

Maddie's heart was racing. "What kind of deal?"

He grinned. "You're going to make this hard on me, aren't you?" His eyes glistened. "Remember I told you that old man Barrett wanted me to make Boston my base?"

Maddie nodded. Her whole body was trembling.

"Well," Michael went on, "I decided it wasn't such a bad idea. I make the switch next month."

Maddie smiled. "I bet that will make your family happy."

"Not as happy as they're going to be when they find out they've got another wedding to plan."

He laughed as he saw the incredulous look on Maddie's face.

"I love you, Maddie."

"Oh, Michael, I love you too. I have from the beginning."

His arms enfolded her. "Did I ever tell you, Maddie Sargent, how terrific you look with a baby in your arms?"

"I do?"

"So what do you say, Maddie? Why don't we get married and have one of our own?"

Maddie felt little pinpricks of happiness travel down her spine. "Only one?"

Michael grinned. It was the warmest, most tender, most loving grin Maddie had ever seen. "Maybe two. Think we can handle two careers, marriage, a couple of kids?"

They looked into each other's eyes and laughed. "Nothing to it," she murmured, kissing him.

HARLEQUIN SIGNATURE EDITION

VIOLET WINSPEAR

HOUSE OF STORMS

Editorial secretary Debra Hartway travels to the Salvador family's
rugged Cornish island home to work on Jack Salvador's latest book.
Disturbing questions hang in the troubled air over Lovelis Island.
What or who had caused the tragic death of Jack's young wife? Why
did Jack stay away from the home and, more especially, the baby
son he loved so well? And—why should Rodare, Jack's brother,
who had proved himself a man of the highest integrity, constantly
invade Debra's thoughts with such passionate, dark desires...?

Violet Winspear, who has written more than 65 romance novels
translated worldwide into 18 languages, is one of Harlequin's best-
loved and bestselling authors. HOUSE OF STORMS, her second title
in the Harlequin Signature Edition program, is a full-length novel
rich in romantic tradition and intriguingly spiced with an atmo-
sphere of danger and mystery.

Watch for HOUSE OF STORMS—coming in October! HOFS-1

Abandon Yourself to

HARLEQUIN *Temptation*®

Harlequin Temptation®
is giving you the chance
to purchase a unique
and sexy nightshirt.

This soft white cotton-polyester nightshirt with Abandon Yourself to Temptation® printed across the front in fiery red, is available to you at a special price.

—**$8.00 with two proofs of purchase from two Harlequin Temptation novels;**

—**$7.00 with three proofs of purchase**

—**$6.00 with five proofs of purchase**

(Retail Value $15.00)

To get your Temptation® nightshirt, clip the special token on this page and send it along with other tokens from your September and October Harlequin Temptation books.

Offer ends December 31, 1988

TO: **HARLEQUIN BOOKS,**
       Temptation Nightshirt Offer,
       901 Fuhrmann Blvd.,
       Box 1396
       Buffalo, New York USA
       14240-9954

YES! I'm ready to abandon myself to Temptation. Please send me my special Harlequin Abandon Yourself To Temptation nightshirt right away.

I am enclosing: ☐ 5 Proofs of Purchase and $6.00
                    ☐ 3 Proofs of Purchase and $7.00
                    ☐ 2 Proofs of Purchase and $8.00

New York and Iowa residents please add sales tax

NAME: _____

ADDRESS: _____

_____

_____

One Size Fits All   Offer Ends December 31, 1988

JOVAN-2-R